Surviving the Storm

Danger in Destiny
Book 8

Melanie D. Snitker

BALLONI MEDIA, LLC

Surviving the Storm
Danger in Destiny: Book 8
By Melanie D. Snitker

Dallionz Media, LLC
P.O. Box 5283
Abilene, TX 79608

Cover Art: Dallionz Media, LLC

Melanie D. Snitker
melanie@melaniedsnitker.com
www.melaniedsnitker.com

For my sweet friend,
Denny Deady.
You are a true inspiration,
and I'm blessed to have
you in my life. Love you!

Chapter One

"I hate thunderstorms." EMT Aurora Graham—or Rory, as she preferred to be called—mumbled from the ambulance's passenger seat. She ducked her head to look out the windshield at the building storm. Some of her copper-colored hair fell, partially obscuring her face.

The dark, billowing clouds in the distance were an ominous backdrop for the flashes of lightning that streaked across the sky. The wind whipped through the branches of nearby trees as the storm drew closer. It was expected to reach Destiny in the next twenty minutes.

Thunder rumbled, startling Rory. She scowled at the sky.

Paramedic Curtis Whitman fastened his seat belt and gripped the ambulance's steering wheel. He felt for Rory. Really, he did. The poor woman jumped every time thunder echoed in the distance.

She also looked adorable. An opinion he wouldn't dare utter aloud.

He was no stranger to the severe weather that frequented Texas every spring and fall. This April had been

1

especially active. While the rain they'd received would go a long way toward increasing the water levels in the lakes nearby, Curtis was ready for a break from the persistent thunderstorms.

"I wonder how long I'll have to live here before I don't have tornado nightmares." Rory kept her gaze on the incoming storm. "It's been over a year, and as soon as spring starts, so do the dreams. Like clockwork."

Curtis chuckled. "Sounds like someone's watched *Twister* one too many times."

She threw him a look that landed somewhere between annoyed and amused. Her rich brown eyes almost matched the color of her hair, which she often wore pulled into a low ponytail. Today, it hung around her shoulders and curled a bit toward the ends.

Details he probably shouldn't have noticed. Then again, he'd found Rory difficult to ignore in general since he met her last year. Considering they often worked together, it was nearly impossible. She was kind, funny, and smart. She also happened to be beautiful. An entirely distracting combination.

Thankfully, he'd managed to bury his interest, especially since they usually worked on the same rig. Thinking about anything but a working relationship would be a disaster.

Except that was all going to change. Curtis hadn't told her yet, but he'd decided to go through the training to work with the local fire department as a paramedic. It wouldn't be easy, but he was looking forward to the challenge.

It would also mean they would no longer be co-workers. Which meant he could ask her out if he wanted to.

The problem was, he didn't think Rory was interested. She'd certainly never given him a single indication that she might be. Then again, she had to be one of the most private people he'd ever known.

He knew she loved chocolate and coconut, that she despised coffee, that she was allergic to peanuts, and that she read books in her spare time. Like, every spare moment.

Thunderstorms rattled her while she took any medical situation they'd faced together with poise and a clear head. Between her ability to focus on the task at hand and her innate ability to put a patient at ease, it was clear that working as a first responder was her calling.

But when it came to her past, her family, and even her reason for choosing to be an EMT, he had no idea. She didn't like to talk about herself much.

He shoved aside the wayward thoughts and focused on what she was saying.

"I'm used to snow after living in Colorado. Tornado watches and hail? I'm not a fan."

As if on cue, a gust of wind whipped around the ambulance and caused it to shake from side to side.

Truthfully, Curtis wasn't a fan of these storms either. But having grown up in Texas, it was just part of spring, like the blooming wildflowers that popped up everywhere this time of year.

He put the rig in gear. "Ready to head back?"

She fastened her seat belt. "Let's do it."

They'd responded to a small accident that'd been called in, but once they got there, no one needed medical assistance, which meant it was time to head back to the hospital again until the next call out. It was Thursday, but it was their equivalent of Friday, so they wouldn't be back on again until eight Sunday morning. Curtis was looking forward to the time off and his niece's birthday party on Saturday.

They'd barely traveled two miles down the narrow two-lane street when they rounded a corner to find two vehicles on the shoulder of the road next to a wire stock fence protecting private property. The black Toyota Corolla looked as though it'd slid passenger-side-first into a tree. A navy-blue pickup truck was parked beside it.

Curtis couldn't tell if the two vehicles had collided at some point or if the driver of the truck had stopped to see if the other driver was okay.

Rory gasped and leaned forward. "I don't see any movement. If this were an old incident, the cars would've been towed by now."

"Agreed." He reached for the radio. "This is unit one. We're approaching the scene of an accident. There's one vehicle involved for sure, possibly a second one. We're stopping and will assess the drivers. We'll need police out here as well." He gave dispatch their location.

"Understood. Contacting DPD. Let us know if you need an additional unit."

"Will do."

Curtis drove the ambulance onto the almost non-existent shoulder and stopped just behind the blue pickup, leaving plenty of room between them. He switched on their emergency lights to make them more visible for anyone else traveling on the road.

He and Rory got their bags of medical gear.

There were still no signs of movement. The whole situation was eerie, and it made him uneasy. He'd feel better if the police were already on the scene. They couldn't wait, though. If someone was injured, those ten minutes could be the difference between life and death.

Rory stared at the car, a hint of hesitation in her eyes.

Curtis bumped her arm with his. "Hey. You okay?"

She swallowed hard. "Yeah. I'll check the car." More lightning and thunder had her casting a furtive look toward the sky.

"I've got the truck. Be careful."

She gave him a subtle nod. A moment of uncertainty flashed in her eyes. Was it because of the storm? Or the situation?

He reached the truck first and looked through the driver's side window. There was no one in either of the front seats, and the door was locked. He couldn't see through the narrow back window very well, so he withdrew his flashlight and illuminated the rear seat, revealing nothing notable.

With a click, Curtis turned the flashlight back off and returned it to his pocket. He walked around the front of the truck. There didn't seem to be any damage to the body. He doubted it was involved in the accident itself.

Wind whipped through the scene as more thunder boomed. It wasn't raining yet, but he could smell it in the air.

"Curtis! We've got a body over here."

Rory's voice was steady, but the tension lacing her tone immediately put him on alert.

He was surprised to find her by the passenger side of the car. She backed away from the door so he could see inside.

A woman was sitting in the passenger seat, her head hanging forward, and her chin nearly touching her chest. Blood trailed from her temple to her chin.

The window had been shattered. Glass littered the ground, just visible in the scraggly grass, and there was some on the woman's lap as well.

The windshield and the driver's side window were

intact. The strangest thing was that there was no one in the driver's seat.

It didn't make much sense.

Rory leaned closer and lowered her voice. "I checked for a pulse. She's dead, but it wasn't the crash that killed her." She reached past him and gently pushed the dead woman back against her seat. "She's been shot."

Curtis's attention snapped to the bullet wound in the victim's chest. Blood soaked the front of her shirt with splatter on the steering wheel and console.

"She was murdered." He had a really bad feeling about this.

Rory swallowed past the lump in her throat. "Was there anyone in the truck?"

"No." Curtis put a hand on her back and turned her toward the ambulance. "I've already called for the police. We need to get somewhere safe while we wait for them to get here."

They began to walk together when she nearly stumbled, her gaze on the tree line. "Someone's watching—"

The words barely left her lips when a sharp crack echoed through the air followed by another as a bullet struck the car mere inches from where Rory was standing.

Chapter Two

I t took a heartbeat or two for Rory to realize the sound was a gunshot and not thunder. Curtis pushed her down low. Together, they crouched and hurried around the back of the car and into the space between it and the truck.

"Stay down." Curtis reached for the radio on his belt. "Dispatch, this is unit one. We're still at the scene of the accident. Gunshots fired. We need assistance immediately. I repeat, we are under fire."

Once dispatch acknowledged his call for help, he clipped the radio back onto his belt. "You saw the shooter?"

She'd been walking next to Curtis when the sensation of being watched dragged her attention to the woods beside them.

There, between two trees, had been the face of a man just barely discernible amid the leaves and branches. Still, it was visible enough to see his eyes narrow as he focused on her. Almost as though he were trying to remember where he knew her from.

She nodded. "It was a man. He was staring at us. What are we going to do?" Rory kept her voice low, her heart pounding in her ears. She got down on her hands and knees and looked under the car. She expected to see shoes on the other side, but there was nothing but brown grass and rocks. "I don't see anyone."

He put a hand on her shoulder. "Listen. We're going to stay low and go around the front of the truck, down the side, and then run to the back end of the ambulance."

Rory rose off the ground and returned to a crouched position. She'd just turned to look at Curtis when another flash of lightning was followed closely by more thunder, loud enough to make the ground vibrate. Wind tossed her hair around and into her face. She pulled it together at the base of her neck and shoved it down the back of her shirt.

Big, fat drops of rain fell from the sky, hitting the dirt and creating mini mud pits. Within moments, it went from sprinkling to a torrent of rain.

"Are you ready?" Curtis asked the question, but he'd already reached for her hand and was making his way to the front of the truck. "Once we start running, don't stop."

Fear coiled in her chest. He tugged her hand, and they were running as fast as they could with their heads below the top of the truck. Even still, Rory was certain she heard another gunshot.

Please, God, get us out of this alive!

The silent prayer screamed in her mind as the combination of cold water and the wind made every raindrop sting the moment it hit her bare skin.

They cleared the pickup truck and were in the open between it and the ambulance when there was another crack, and this time she knew it was a gunshot.

Curtis hissed but kept pulling her along with him until they were next to the back, left tire of the ambulance.

The rain, which reduced visibility, kept coming down in sheets. The wind whipped through, changing the direction of the downpour like a school of fish changing direction in the sea.

Rory shivered and braced herself. Would the shooter follow them? Kill them both since they'd stumbled on the scene of a murder that she could only assume the shooter was responsible for.

Sirens cut through the storm, faint at first, then gaining strength. Before they could see the welcoming red and blue lights, the pickup truck pulled away from the shoulder with a squeal of the tires and tore off down the street.

Sharp relief hit Rory, and she leaned against the side of the ambulance. A flash of lightning preceded thunder that she barely noticed.

Curtis turned and positioned himself in front of her. "Are you okay? Were you hit?" His gaze combed her body, looking for injuries.

"No. I'm okay."

She was about to ask him the same question when she noticed a tear in his uniform just above his elbow. The flesh she could barely see inside was bloody, and blood dripped from the fingers of that same hand. "Curtis! You're hurt."

He shook his head. "I think it just grazed me. The rain is making the blood look worse than it is."

Two police cars neared and pulled off the side of the road. One officer immediately set up flares to help passing cars see the accident from a distance. Another officer Rory had met before—Clint Baker—approached them at a jog.

"What's the situation. Are the two of you okay?"

"We're going to be fine." Curtis pointed to the car. "There's a deceased female in the passenger seat of the car. GSW. We never saw the driver. There's one shooter that we know of—Rory saw him in the woods. He drove away in that truck just as you arrived."

Officer Baker gave a sharp nod. "Understood. It might be best if you both get into the back of the ambulance and wait while we clear the scene." With that, he walked off.

Rory could just hear him asking for officers to be on the lookout for the truck and its last known location.

"He's right. You need to get inside and dry off." Curtis looked pointedly at her hands.

Only then did Rory realize they were shaking. Her whole body was shaking. "I think it's more of an adrenaline thing."

He didn't disagree, so he led the way to the back of the ambulance and opened the doors. They both climbed inside.

Rory sat down hard on one of the benches with a groan. She clasped her hands together, willing them to stop shaking. She needed to look at Curtis's arm and make sure it wasn't more than just the flesh wound he thought it was.

Curtis opened one of the storage compartments and pulled out two emergency blankets. He unfolded one and draped it over Rory's shoulders before using one himself. She wasn't sure either of them had a dry stitch of clothing on them.

She clutched the corners of her blanket beneath her chin. "Do you think the shooter would've kept trying to kill us if the police hadn't arrived when they did?"

"Maybe. Or it's possible they were really just trying to clear the way to get into their truck before officers arrived. If they murdered the woman in the car, obviously they wouldn't want to get caught."

She'd like to think that the driver of the truck would've taken off when they reached the back of the ambulance, whether the police had shown up or not. The idea that they might have been minutes away from being shot was too much to focus on.

Her thoughts drifted back to the guy she saw. There was something about the way the guy had just stared at her. She suppressed a shudder and focused. "I need to take a look at your arm."

Curtis looked like he was going to protest. Instead, he shrugged off the blanket and unbuttoned his uniform shirt to reveal a black undershirt. He pulled his right arm out of the sleeve and winced.

Blood stained his arm from the wound above his elbow all the way down to his fingers. Curtis was right, though. The rainwater had diluted the blood to make it look worse than it actually was.

Rory abandoned her own blanket and started to get the first aid supplies out. "Between this and the bombing at the courthouse in December, I can't imagine choosing to run into danger for a living."

She started to use alcohol swabs to clean his wound and wipe the blood off his arm and hand. Even though he had to be freezing, too, his arm felt warm against her icy hands. If he noticed, he didn't react or complain. He studied her for a minute, his expression unreadable. If he was going to say something, he seemed to think better of it.

Rory focused on his wound. "You're right, the bullet just grazed you. No stitches required." She spread antibiotic cream onto a piece of gauze, placed it over the injury, and then secured it with medical tape. "It was close, Curtis. Way too close."

"Yeah, it was." He slipped his arm back into his uniform shirt and buttoned it again. "Thanks for taking care of it."

"You're welcome." She sat back down again and reached for her emergency blanket.

He opened another storage compartment and withdrew a couple of heating packs. He tore one open and handed it to her. Rory pressed it between her palms as it started to heat up.

After opening another for himself, he sat down again.

Rory stilled and listened. The storm must have passed over them because she couldn't remember the last time she heard thunder. Rain was still coming down, the drops pattering on the roof of the ambulance.

Curtis cleared his throat. "If it hadn't started to rain when it did..."

It'd probably made it harder for the shooter to see and aim properly after that first shot. If it hadn't been raining, things likely would've been so much worse.

"It was definitely a Godsend."

He gave a short nod. "That it was."

Rory was cold and nervous as they waited for the police to let them know everything was safe. Finally, there was a knock at the large door.

"It's Officer Baker. We're clear out here."

Curtis got to his feet, opened the door, and motioned for the officer to come in out of the rain. "Were you able to find the driver from the car?"

If they had, he or she might need medical attention.

Baker sat down on the bench seat next to Curtis. "We did. Unfortunately, he was already deceased. We've got a

BOLO out on the blue pickup. Did either of you happen to see the license plate number, or even a partial?"

"No." Curtis frowned. "We were focused on locating the drivers and making sure they were okay. I've got to say, though, that I may snap photos of license plates from now on. I wish I had today."

"I didn't notice either." Rory tucked the emergency blanket around her legs.

Curtis described the truck he'd seen. With as wet as the ground was outside, hopefully there would be tire tracks for the forensics team to check out. Assuming the rain didn't wash them away.

Officer Baker wrote down every detail. "Could you tell if there was more than one shooter? Did you see them?"

"I only heard one gun. It sounded like a .38. There were two, maybe three shots." Curtis started to raise his arm to scratch the back of his neck, but it must have been painful because he dropped his injured arm again. "Rory spotted him in the woods."

Baker turned his attention to Rory. "Can you give a description of the man you saw?"

It'd all happened so fast. She closed her eyes and tried to replay it in her mind. "I think he was crouched or ducked down. I don't know how tall he was. White. Lighter colored eyes. I don't know what color, but they weren't brown."

"Did he have any facial hair? Anything distinguishing about his face?"

"No facial hair. I didn't see him well enough to notice scars or anything like that." Her eyes flew open. "I was watching him up until the gunshot. If he shot at us, he didn't have the gun up by his face to aim."

"Which means there may have been more than one

assailant." Concern tugged at the corners of the officer's mouth.

It was a miracle neither of them had been killed.

Thank you, God.

The man in the woods had likely been watching them since they'd arrived on the scene. Would she recognize him if they crossed paths again? Would he recognize her? The thought sent another chill down her spine.

Chapter Three

Curtis wasn't sure if Rory was ever going to stop shivering. He was certain that was why Officer Baker encouraged them to head back to the hospital to change clothes and said he'd stop by in an hour or two with an update and to get their official statements. The officer was probably hoping Rory might remember more about the man she saw if she were warmer and in a safer environment.

Thankfully, they both had a change of clothes waiting for them back at the hospital. Once Rory was in dry clothing and had a cup of hot coffee in her hands, the pink color started to return to her fingers.

Karen Beltway, the director of the EMS department at the hospital and their boss, was waiting for them when they arrived at the hospital. Her hair, which was a dark blonde mixed with gray, was pulled into a tight bun at the back of her head. It gave her a stern look to match her no-nonsense personality.

After making sure they were okay, the first thing she did

was arrange for Curtis to have his arm looked at again. Rory had done a fine job, but Karen insisted that it was necessary for insurance purposes.

Of course, the nurses and doctor in the ER agreed it was superficial and wouldn't need stitches before patching him up again.

He returned to the waiting room to find Rory and Karen watching for him. He gave his boss the full report.

"If you need time off—either of you—it can certainly be arranged." She pinned Rory with a meaningful stare. "You haven't taken a single day since you started working here. I hope you'll submit a request soon."

Rory nodded but didn't look pleased. "I'll check my calendar and try to get some dates for you."

"In the meantime, make yourselves comfortable in one of the family rooms. We'll be sure to let the police know where you are. Hopefully, they can finish their questioning so you can both go home and get some rest. And let me know about that time off." She gave them a pointed look and headed out, her high-heeled shoes click-clacking on the tile well after she was no longer visible.

Curtis motioned for Rory to follow him. "Come on, the family room is probably warmer anyway. I just need to grab some coffee myself."

A few minutes later, they were sitting around a table in the small room with their drinks. He'd hoped the room would be warmer, but if it was, the difference was negligible. He pulled his cell phone out of his pocket.

"This is going to end up on the news, and I'd rather give my parents a heads up so they don't hear about the incident and wonder if we were involved. It'll just be a few minutes."

She nodded for him to go ahead.

Curtis dialed his dad's number. "Hey, Pop. Rory and I are both fine, but there was an incident tonight." He relayed the situation with as few details as possible, reassuring both his dad and mom that he really was okay. "Yeah. I'm not sure how long it'll take to go over the details, but I promise I'll stop by before I head back home. Absolutely. Love you, too."

He hung up the phone and watched Rory as she stared at the contents of her cup.

"Do you need to call anyone?"

She blinked at her coffee before looking up. It took a second or two for his question to register with her.

"Sorry. No, I don't need to call anyone."

"I suppose your family in Colorado isn't likely to hear anything from the news here in Destiny." He paused, hoping she might give a little more information about her family. When she stayed silent, he changed the subject. "When was the last time you took a vacation? Like a real one where you traveled somewhere?"

She seemed to think about that for a minute, then smiled. "It was when I moved to Texas, actually. I took almost two weeks to get here, and went through Utah, Arizona, New Mexico, and then into Texas. I figured it might be my last chance to do something like that for a while."

"That's awesome. What was your favorite stop?"

"I loved Lake Powell. Everything about it, from the Rainbow Bridge to the Glen Canyon Dam. It was just beautiful and so colorful. I ended up staying three days there before I could make myself move on. Honestly, I thought the Grand Canyon would be my favorite. I guess that's what makes exploring so much fun."

"Did you stay in hotels?"

"I pulled a small trailer. Made it easy to stop at any of the state parks along the way."

He wanted to ask if she'd made the trip alone, but he instinctively knew she had. "That sounds amazing, Rory. Good for you. Do you think you'd make a trip like that again in the future?"

"I hope so." There was an enthusiastic lilt to her voice, but her eyes held doubt. "What about you? Anywhere you've dreamed of traveling to?"

"I've always wanted to go to Yellowstone and to see the Great Lakes. Separate trips, most likely." He shrugged. "I've lived in Texas my whole life, and family trips were almost always within five hours of home. Getting out and exploring is definitely on my to-do list."

"Having so much family in town would make it hard to leave for long." There was no missing the longing in her words.

"It does, but I wouldn't change it for anything." His older sisters were all married and had kids. Curtis loved being the fun uncle, but someday, he wanted a family of his own.

If he ever met "the one."

It's not like he had a great track record when it came to women. After all, he'd thought he'd found her a few years ago. Georgia had been beautiful and smart but tended to avoid the truth. A fact he didn't know until it was too late. Learning that she was no longer in love with him a week before their wedding had been a difficult reality to deal with.

Rory was the first woman since Georgia that he'd had any interest in. No matter how much he tried to get to know her, it always seemed like she had something to hide. Maybe it was because she was an overly private person. But after what happened with Georgia, he wasn't sure he wanted to put himself in that position again. He wanted to get involved with someone he could trust—and who trusted him in return.

Sometimes it felt like too much to ask.

There was a knock on the door a moment before it opened. Officer Baker's face appeared. "Someone told me you two were in here. Mind if I come in?"

"Not at all." Curtis motioned to one of the free chairs around the circular table they were sitting at. "There's some coffee just outside. I can grab you a cup."

"Nah. I've never been a coffee drinker." He took a seat. "Thanks, though."

"Not a problem. Any updates? Were you able to track down the truck?"

"We found it about five miles away, abandoned in a ditch on the side of the road. It'd been torched. We ran the plates, but it was reported stolen a county over two days ago. Forensics will go over what's left with a fine-toothed comb, but the likelihood of finding prints or any other evidence is small."

"That's unfortunate." Rory frowned. "They had to have had a way to leave the area after burning the truck."

Baker nodded. "That's what we're thinking, too. Unfortunately, that section of road is pretty remote. No cameras. But tech is going through footage from either side of it. We're hoping they might catch something."

"Any identification on the victims?" Curtis could still picture the woman in the passenger seat, the bullet wound in her chest. "Was the victim in the woods shot, too?"

"It was a married couple. And yes, he'd been shot as well. Multiple times. The investigation is still ongoing, so I can't share all the details at this point. Detective Nate Walker will be taking the case on. I'm gathering information for him now."

They spent the following half hour or more going over their statements again.

Baker made several notes and asked multiple questions. Curtis used a finger to trace the outline of the bandage on his arm as he answered them with as many details as he could.

The officer turned to focus on Rory. "I know you gave us a description of the man you saw. If some names were to come up during the investigation, do you think you would recognize him if you saw his picture?"

Rory nibbled on one corner of her bottom lip for a moment or two. "I'm not sure. Maybe. Everything happened so fast."

"It's okay. There's no pressure. Sometimes, when something like this happens, people find they remember more later. When they're more relaxed or even right after waking up. If that does happen to either of you, please be sure to reach out." Baker handed each of them a business card.

Rory took her card. "When I spotted the man in the woods, he was staring at me. Like, really staring. I know I've seen way too many crime shows, and I'm probably just being paranoid, but I have to ask. Do we need to worry about this guy trying to track me down because I might recognize him if I saw him again?"

"It's highly unlikely. After committing a double homicide and burning the stolen vehicle, they're probably long gone by now." The officer paused. "However, if there's someone you can stay with, it wouldn't hurt. As much as to put your mind at ease as anything. I can also arrange to have patrols go by your homes regularly at night until we catch them."

Curtis knew enough about Rory to guess she wouldn't consider staying with someone else. He wished she would, because the idea of her remaining at the RV park with that guy out there somewhere made Curtis more than a little uneasy.

Chapter Four

It was clear Rory was nervous about the idea that the men from the crime scene could be anywhere. Curtis wasn't surprised when she agreed to the extra patrols. But when Officer Baker asked for her address and they found out she lived in the RV park on the far edge of town, both men tried to convince her to stay in a hotel or somewhere a little closer to town.

She insisted that it wasn't necessary, and from her shuttered expression, it was clear she had no intention of changing her mind.

As for Curtis, at least the house he owned was armed with a security system. How protected could Rory's trailer be?

After Baker left, they let Karen know they were heading out as well, and they walked together to the employee parking lot. It was just after six, and the sun was shining as though there hadn't been a thunderstorm earlier. They still had about two hours of daylight left. The temperature was pleasant, even if it was a little humid.

They'd parked their vehicles just a few spaces apart.

Rory tipped her head toward his blue Jeep Wrangler. "The rubber ducks on your dashboard always make me smile."

He grinned at the colorful conglomerate. "Me, too. Most of them are from my nieces and nephews. Whenever they find a new one somewhere, they always have to get it for me for my birthday or Christmas. There are too many to display, so I rotate every so often."

"That's a fun tradition." She eyed the ducks for another moment before jabbing her thumb in the direction of her van. "I'd better get going."

Her Dodge van was old and had several areas where the gray paint had been scraped off and some rust was settling in. He'd never seen her drive anything but it. Still, even with the damage, it seemed to be in good shape.

"Are you sure I can't convince you to get a hotel or something for a few days?"

"I'm sure." She studied him. "I appreciate your concern, though. Truthfully, I'm living in my trailer until I can afford a house. I'm not too far away, and I don't really want to blow money on a hotel and push that date back. Especially when the guys are likely long gone. What if it takes the police two weeks to track them down?"

Rory made a good point. She stood facing him, her spine straight and her arms crossed in front of her as though she were daring him to contradict her.

"I totally get it." Curtis gave her a reassuring smile. "Well, it's not every day that we get shot at. If you get home and want to talk about it, don't hesitate to give me a call. Okay?"

"Yeah." Her hand dropped to her sides. "Thanks. Same to you. Here's to an uneventful evening for both of us."

"Amen."

Curtis got into his Jeep and watched as Rory drove her vehicle out of the parking lot. Even though he was desperate for a hot shower, he stopped by his parents' house first.

Stanley and Grace Whitman had been married for over forty years, and their dedication to each other and their family was something Curtis admired. The two were each other's best friend, and that's the kind of relationship he wanted, too.

They lived in a house on the other side of Destiny—the same house that Curtis grew up in. Even though he hadn't lived there in years, it always felt like going home again. And with all of his sisters and their families, he also never knew who was going to be there. Today, though, it was quiet.

Mom answered the door and ushered him in with a tight hug. There was no way to tell which arm was injured since he wore a shirt over the bandage, so she made sure to be careful with both of them.

"Your father and I were worried, but we're glad you called us to let us know what happened."

Pop came into the room and gave him a hug. "Not knowing and hearing stuff on the news is always more worrisome."

It was his way of telling Curtis that he did the right thing by keeping them in the loop.

"I'm okay. It was just a graze and should heal up fine. No one else was hurt." At least no one responding to the scene. He wasn't going to go into details about the victims. For one thing, it was an ongoing case. For another, Mom had a way of spreading news through the family like wildfire. And even if she would make sure not to share with someone outside the family, there was no guarantee everyone else would do the same.

"Glad to hear it, son."

"We're eating late tonight." Mom motioned toward the kitchen. "I just put a lasagna in the oven. It'll be about an hour. Do you want to stay and eat?"

Curtis shook his head. "As delicious as that sounds, I'm exhausted. I need to go home, shower, and get some rest."

He wondered what Rory was doing right now. Hopefully, she had the chance to wind down a little and get some sleep. But no matter what he did, he couldn't get the fact that she was living in a trailer out of his mind. There was nothing wrong with that. Trailers and RVs were great, and it made sense to live in one while saving up for a house. He just couldn't picture the RV park as anything but this dark area far from town.

"Was Rory shaken up?" Mom's question caught Curtis off guard. He blinked at her, wondering how she knew he'd been thinking about his co-worker.

"Yeah, she was. We both were. I'm glad things like this aren't the norm."

"Oh, we are, too." Mom wrapped her arms around Curtis in a tight hug. "Thanks for stopping by. And we'll see you on Saturday for Belle's party."

"I wouldn't miss it." His niece was turning seven. "Love you guys. Talk to you later."

Curtis gave them each another hug and headed back to his Jeep.

He drove home, got a hot shower, and then started looking through his fridge for something to eat. For the tenth time, his thoughts shifted to Rory. Before he could overthink it, he picked up his phone and dialed her number.

She picked up on the second ring. "Hey, Curtis. Is everything okay?" She sounded surprised.

Of course, he'd never called her before. Texted when he was running late, or in response to one of hers, sure.

"Yeah, I'm good. Hey, I'm exhausted and have nothing to eat at my house. I thought I might grab a pizza. Is there any chance I could convince you to let me swing by and share it with you?"

There was a moment of silence, and Curtis looked at the screen on his phone to make sure they hadn't been disconnected.

"I don't know. My place is a mess. After everything today, I'm kind of a mess."

That brought a smile to his face. "That doesn't matter. Trust me, I'm not going to judge. I'm just going to bring a supreme pizza, we'll eat, and then I'll get out of your hair."

Curtis sat in front of his computer and pulled up the website for his favorite pizza place. He started the order.

She'd told him numerous times how much she liked supreme pizza, especially with extra olives, which was exactly how he intended to order it.

"Come on, Rory. I can eat a whole pizza by myself, but that doesn't mean I should. Save me from myself."

A quiet chuckle came across the line. "Fine. Thank you." She told him the address and site number, although he remembered when she gave the information to Officer Baker.

"You're welcome. I'll see you in about thirty minutes."

He got his handgun out of the small safe on his side table, slipped it into the holster, and tucked it into the back of his jeans. He wished he'd had it earlier when they were being shot at.

The pizza place said his order would be ready in twenty. The timing would be perfect.

Once he collected it, he headed for the RV park where Rory was staying. It wasn't quite dark yet, but the sun was well into setting.

What his dad said earlier about not knowing a situation making a person worry more came to mind. He truly hoped he'd get to the RV park and find it was well-lit with a lot of people staying at it. That way, he wouldn't worry as much about Rory being out so far and alone.

This park ranked somewhere in the middle. The office area was well lit along with the public restrooms and laundry room. The further away he got from that central location, the fewer streetlights he saw. He imagined that, when it came to some of the side streets, drivers relied heavily on their headlights and the reflectors on the vehicles and trailers as guides to stay on the narrow, caliche roads.

Space 301 was toward the back at the end of one of the streets. There wasn't a streetlight down there. As Curtis's Jeep approached, the headlights caught Rory's van parked in front of a small trailer. He'd guess it to be sixteen feet long. Maybe eighteen. The trailer looked older, just like her van, but it seemed to be in good condition.

There was no room to park behind her van, so he went around the other side to park beside it on the gravel. As he did, his headlights illuminated the shape of a person standing outside one of the trailer windows on the back side, as though trying to look in.

Curtis threw his Jeep into park and opened the door. "Hey! What're you doing out there?"

The outline of the person paused, seemed to think through the options, and then took off running in the opposite direction. He started to pursue, but by the time he got to the other side of the trailer, the peeping Tom had disappeared into the darkness.

Chapter Five

Rory heard a vehicle approaching outside and was opening a curtain to see if it was Curtis when she heard his raised voice.

"Hey! What're you doing out there?"

A faint scuffle sounded from outside the window next to the little dinette, followed by the pounding of footsteps.

With a knot in her throat, she waited until there was a knock at the door. "Rory? It's Curtis."

She opened it outward, careful not to hit him. "What's going on?"

He was standing on packed ground at the base of the stairs leading into her trailer. He glanced to his left and then focused on her.

"Someone was trying to look in your window when I pulled up."

The scuffling sound. She knew which window Curtis was talking about. "Were you able to see who it was?"

"No. It was too dark. I'm positive it was a man, but that's about it." He pointed to his Jeep. "Let me grab a flashlight, and we'll go take a look. Make sure your window wasn't tampered with."

She nodded. "I'll get my shoes."

By the time she slipped them on and exited her trailer, Curtis had already retrieved his flashlight and was waiting for her. Together, they walked around to the window.

It was silly, but Rory had to tuck her hands in her pockets to keep from reaching out and touching his arm. Having him there made her feel safer, and it was almost impossible not to want to draw some of that from him.

The beam from his light lit up the ground. While this area of town had received some rain earlier in the day, it wasn't the downpour they'd experienced at the accident scene. Still, the ground was wet enough to display footprints where someone had once been standing.

Curtis handed her the flashlight. "Here, I'm going to take pictures of these. I'll send them, along with a description of what happened, to Officer Baker. I doubt it has anything to do with before, but if you've got someone sneaking around your place, the police should be aware of it. Especially if any other people staying here have had similar experiences."

"That's a good idea." She kept the flashlight on the footprints so Curtis could kneel and get a close-up picture. "I'll ask around tomorrow. See if anyone else has seen any suspicious activity or had anything go missing."

Curtis stood, sent a text with several pictures, pocketed his phone, and took the flashlight again. "Have you had problems with anyone before?"

"We get raccoons that mess with the trash at night. Every once in a while, someone hosts a party, and it goes on later than I'd prefer. But other than that, it's been a decent place to stay."

"That's good. Hopefully it was random, and nearly being caught will discourage him from doing something like that again."

"I sure hope that's the case." Rory swallowed and tried to ignore the unease in the pit of her stomach. "I'm glad you drove up when you did."

"Me, too." For the first time since he arrived, Curtis smiled. "Come on, I have a pizza in the passenger seat with our names on it."

As she led him inside, suddenly, the thought of him seeing the inside of her trailer made her nervous. She tried to imagine it from a stranger's vantage point. Sure, it was picked up. That wasn't what she was worried about. It was an older trailer, and while it was clean, it wasn't as nice looking as the newer models. It didn't have all the fancy bells and whistles, and that included a functioning built-in air conditioner. Instead, she had a window unit placed above the sink. It was enough to keep the small living space cooler in the summer.

"Here, you can set the pizza on the table. Can I get you something to drink?" Rory opened the fridge. "I've got some bottled water and Sprite." With such a small refrigerator, there wasn't a lot of room for variety. She usually limited it to drinks, milk for cereal, and sandwich meat.

"I'll take a water. Thank you."

It was impossible not to worry what Curtis might think about her trailer. She told herself it didn't matter, but that was a lie. Well, it was where she lived now, and it was hers. Not everyone could say that.

She'd always figured she'd save up enough money for a down payment on a little house. Something she owned herself. Now, after everything today, she was considering the possibility of renting a place instead. She could probably manage that if she didn't mind that it'd be years before she could afford to buy a home of her own.

Rory handed him the water, and they took a seat.

"I like the pictures." Curtis pointed to the limited wall space behind the dinette table. "Postcards?"

"I stopped and got one every chance I had on the drive from Colorado."

She shouldn't have been worried, though. They got to talking about the places she'd visited as they ate. If he had any negative thoughts about where she lived, he kept them to himself.

"This pizza is *so* good." The more toppings on a pizza the better, as far as she was concerned. "Thanks for offering to bring it. Though you could've gone with pepperoni. That would've been delicious, too."

Pepperoni was Curtis's favorite. Until now, she didn't even know he liked supreme.

"I'm not sure I've met a pizza I didn't like. Besides, I figured I'd better up the ante if you were going to agree to let me come by." His brown eyes twinkled.

"Clever."

"Was I wrong?"

Rory tried to think of a witty comeback, but she was just too tired. Finally, she shook her head. "Nope, you weren't wrong."

He laughed loudly at her honesty, the rumble filling her trailer and making her smile.

It was nice not eating alone for a change.

She motioned to his wounded arm. "How's it feeling?"

"Truthfully? I'm looking forward to taking some Tylenol tonight." He flexed it. "I can tell it'll be sore for a few days, but nothing horrible. I'm going to talk to Karen tomorrow. I want to return to work after our seventy-two off. I don't think I need more time than that. What about you? Have you thought about it yet?"

"Same. I don't need to take extra time off. Besides, if I schedule vacation, it's going to be for something planned and fun." At the moment, she couldn't even think of what that would be. "I'll call her tomorrow, too."

"Sounds good." He polished off the last bite of his pizza and looked longingly at the slices that were still left. "My eyes want more, but my stomach says I've had enough."

"I hear you." She popped an olive slice in her mouth. "Thanks again for bringing this by."

"Of course." He looked like he was about to say something else when his phone chimed. He scrolled to the texts. "It's from Baker. He says they got several shoe prints from the accident earlier today. They'll compare them to the ones we sent over just to cover their bases. They're also going to look into reports from the area. See if anyone else has had issues with people peeping around their places. In the meantime, he's assured me that you'll have a patrol going by regularly tonight."

"I appreciate that." She truly did. But the guy Curtis caught in the act had been on the opposite side of her trailer from the road. A police officer wouldn't have seen him from the patrol car anyway.

When she'd first moved into the RV park, she'd chosen this particular spot because it was away from the main road and the office. Now she wished she'd chosen one in a more central location. Maybe she'd speak with the manager tomorrow and get it moved. It'd be a pain, but it was certainly doable.

Curtis leaned back and studied her. "Are you sure you wouldn't be more comfortable staying in a hotel for a day or two? I know you said that you're good with going back to work in a few days, but you could take some vacation. Go to Colorado and stay with family for a few days."

Rory didn't like talking about her family with anyone. It was a part of her past, and she preferred to leave it there. She considered deflecting, but there was Curtis, watching her with such concern. It meant a lot. She couldn't remember the last time someone had been so worried about her. The back of her eyelids burned with tears she refused to shed.

"I don't have any family."

Chapter Six

No family at all? Curtis had such a large one himself and couldn't imagine birthdays or holidays without a whole slew of people there to celebrate together. His sisters had driven him crazy many times, but he wouldn't change that for anything.

He had so many questions, but he didn't want to push more than he already had. Instead, he leaned back in his chair and took a drink of his water. Letting her know that he was there to listen.

Rory was watching him, an expression on her face that he couldn't quite read. Was she trying to decide how he might react if she said what was on her mind? Or maybe she was trying to come up with a polite way to ask him to leave and not come back.

With the kind of sigh that spoke of a weariness that cut to the bone, she slowly shifted her gaze from him to her can of soda. "I was an only child and never had extended family that was a part of my life."

She reached for the can and shook it gently. There must

not have been anything left in it because she set it down again.

"My parents struggled with addiction for as long as I can remember. When I was twelve, my mom had too much to drink. She and my dad got in a huge argument, so she insisted I get in the car and she drove us toward town. I don't know if she planned to leave him for good or if she was just trying to make a statement. Hasty decisions like that weren't unusual for either of them when they were angry with each other."

She picked up her napkin and crumpled it into a ball that she tucked into her closed hand. "We were in the middle of a severe thunderstorm and driving along a street that didn't have much lighting. Our car ran off the road and hit a tree. My mom was killed instantly. The police said she'd passed out at the wheel and lost control."

Curtis's stomach clenched, and a sick feeling settled there like a rock. "Rory... I can't imagine. I'm so sorry. Were you hurt?"

Her chin lifted, and the sadness in her amber eyes mixed with a wariness he couldn't possibly understand.

She turned her head toward him and swept her hair away from her ear. A jagged scar ran along the hairline from the top of her right ear to nearly the nape of her neck.

How had he never noticed it before? She'd probably come up with hairstyles that hid it perfectly.

"The doctors said it was a miracle I survived, and even more so that I walked away without any permanent brain damage."

"I'm so glad that you did."

She gave a subtle nod and brushed her hair back in place, hiding the scar. She dropped the crumpled napkin on her plate, where it slowly unfurled.

He thought back on the accident earlier, and his heart ached. Seeing that the car had slid into a tree with a thunderstorm looming had to have been difficult for Rory.

"What about your dad?"

"He cleaned himself up and got a job." Her voice caught. "I used to imagine what it would be like to have a dad who did things with me. It was like a dream come true. He took me to school, came to my plays, and we even ate dinner together. But a year later, he lost his job. He turned to alcohol again. I think it was always there. Taunting him." She shrugged. "I'd been taking care of myself for the most part before that anyway. I was used to it."

It took a great deal of control to keep his expression neutral. The idea that a man could leave his grieving daughter on her own was appalling. He sent up a silent prayer of thanks that she managed to survive her childhood, and another for his own amazing parents.

No child should be used to taking care of themselves. He had a feeling there were many times she probably took care of her father, too.

"Where's your dad now?"

Another shrug as though it didn't matter, but Curtis knew that was far from the truth.

"He died two years ago. Liver disease. When he went in to have his gallbladder removed, there were complications. He never made it out of surgery."

A new level of respect surged through Curtis. He could hardly fathom what she must have gone through, and yet, here she was. Dedicated to a job that helped others. He'd seen nothing but kindness and empathy from her when it came to dealing with the people they saw daily. People who were facing their own crises and relied on them for help.

He wanted to ask her why she chose to work as an

EMT, but didn't want to push too hard on the more personal stuff. She'd already revealed more to him today than she had in the last year he'd known her.

"What brought you to Destiny of all places?"

Pink flooded her cheeks. "It's actually pretty silly."

"I promise I won't tell anyone."

That earned him a raised eyebrow. "I'm going to hold you to that, Whitman."

He lifted his hands, palms out.

"I wanted to move somewhere different—some place where I could start over completely. When I settled on Texas, I started looking at small towns. I don't know, as soon as I saw Destiny listed, I knew it was the one. I guess I hoped I'd find my own way here somehow."

She glanced away, clearly embarrassed.

Starting over somewhere new was probably what she needed the most. He gave her an encouraging smile. "And of all the towns you might have chosen in Texas, I'm glad you picked Destiny."

"I am, too." A small smile played at the corners of her mouth. She stood and started to gather the trash.

"Why don't you keep the leftovers? If you have enough room, that is." She had one of those small fridges that you normally saw in travel trailers. Even though she'd retrieved a drink for each of them earlier, he hadn't noticed how full it was.

"Are you sure?" Her eyes brightened at the idea.

"Absolutely."

"Thank you." She gave him another bright smile. Together, they wrapped the leftover pizza in plastic for her to put up. Her small trash was full, so he offered to run it down to the dumpster that he'd seen at the end of the road.

By the time he got back, she was sitting at the picnic table on the grassy area beside her trailer.

Half of her face was in the shadows while the porch light on her trailer lit the other half in a harsh glow. She covered a yawn with one hand.

That was his cue to leave so she could get some rest. Man, he hated leaving her here, though. "Are you sure I can't talk you into staying at a hotel?"

"I'm sure." She looked at the trailer over her shoulder. "I know it's not much, but it's home."

It wasn't hard to read between the lines. This place was all she had, and she wasn't about to walk away from it for any reason. He could respect that.

"Would it be okay if I sent a text in the morning to check in?

A ghost of a smile appeared, almost as though she were trying to suppress it. "I'd appreciate that."

Curtis smiled in response. "Good. And if you need anything, please don't hesitate to text or call me either, okay? I'm awake early. Seriously, by six in the morning like clockwork." He tipped his head toward her trailer. "Now I'll wait until you get inside and lock the door before I head out."

She chuckled as she stood. "Have a good night, Curtis. I hope the arm feels better in the morning."

"Thanks. Get some rest."

He waited until he heard the click of her lock before heading back to his Jeep. Even after he started the engine, he had a hard time making himself leave. It wasn't until the curtains parted and he saw her peeking out that he figured he'd better go before she accused *him* of being a stalker. With a quick wave, he put the Jeep in drive and started home.

"Father, please place a hedge of protection around Rory and her place. Keep her safe. Please guide Officer Baker and the others as they locate the murderers." He paused, and gratitude filled his heart when he thought of how much worse today could've been. "Thank you for helping Rory and me get out of that situation in one piece."

Even though Curtis slept relatively well that night, he still woke up several times due to pain in his arm. Each time, he glanced at his phone and made sure he hadn't missed a call or text from Rory. By five the next morning, he was wide awake, dressed, and feeling antsy. Taking a hot shower and putting a fresh dressing on his arm didn't take up nearly as much time as he thought it should. He kept himself busy catching up on e-mails, paying some bills, and wrapping his niece's birthday gift. Despite her name, Belle was more into Minecraft than Disney princesses. He hoped she'd love what he got her.

It was nearly eight when a text came through from Rory.

> Good morning. I hope your arm is feeling better today.

> A little, thanks. Did you get some rest?

> I slept better than I thought I would. But I woke up to a problem.

Curtis was instantly on alert.

> What happened?

> Someone slashed the tires on my van.

Chapter Seven

Rory had no more than sent her text telling Curtis that her tires had been slashed when her phone rang. His concern and lack of hesitation to call might have made her smile if the situation were different.

"Did you call the police and report the slashed tires? Was it all four of them?"

"Yes, it was all four. I called as soon as I saw them. Someone took the report, then maybe two minutes later, Officer Baker called me. He said he's coming over to look at everything here shortly and advised me to not touch the tires. He said there may be prints."

There were muffled sounds coming from Curtis's end of the call. "I'm glad he's going to come in person. If you have no objections, I'd like to be there as well."

"Please don't feel like you have to come over. But if you want to, that would be great."

"Of course." There was a trace of relief in his voice as a door closed in the background. "I'm heading your way now."

It was kind of him to want to be there when Baker came

by. That Curtis offered didn't surprise Rory in the least. What she didn't see coming was the immediate relief she felt knowing he was on his way.

"I just wish I knew if the tires had been slashed before the guy was messing with my window or if he came back later and did it. Or if it was someone else entirely."

The thought of someone sneaking around outside her trailer for the second time gave her the heebie-jeebies. She'd been able to go to sleep last night despite everything. She doubted it would be so easy tonight.

"I wish we knew, too. I never even paid much attention to your van when I got there. I'd like to think I'd have noticed flat tires, but I can't be sure."

They chatted about different theories and unrelated things until he pulled up to her trailer a little over ten minutes later.

Rory had been sitting inside watching for him. She met him outside as he exited his Jeep. He reached out and gave her upper arm a gentle squeeze. It was such a little thing, but she allowed herself to relish the comfort the action brought her.

Curtis led the way to her van for a look at the tires. "Man, whoever did this wanted to make sure you weren't going anywhere."

"No joke." Each tire had several wide punctures in it. It wasn't like someone just jabbed it once and ran off. Ugh, how was she supposed to get the tires replaced? If it were just one flat, she could take it to a tire store. But this... She was going to have to hire a tow truck. Just what she didn't need.

Rory didn't often think about her dad and wish that he were still alive, or think about what it would've been like if he'd stayed sober. But right now, it would've been nice to have him here to take care of her.

"Here's Officer Baker."

Curtis's announcement gave Rory what she needed to put an end to her pity party. Nothing good came from mourning what never was.

"Good morning." Baker offered his hand to each of them. "Sorry to see you guys again so soon under these circumstances." He folded his arms in front of his chest as he took in her flat tires.

"Thanks for coming out." Curtis motioned to her van. "We aren't sure whether this happened around the same time the prowler was here, or if this was a separate incident."

Baker pulled a notebook from his front pocket. "I looked through all the reports filed by residents and guests at this park, and all that comes up are several noise complaints and a couple of calls over people driving at excessive speeds." He flipped to another page. "There was a break-in about two miles down the road. Some electronics were stolen, and the perpetrator hasn't been caught yet. There were three different incidences of vehicle vandalism, but that individual was apprehended."

Rory frowned.

Truthfully, she'd been hoping that what happened to her van was part of a string of incidents. Not that she wanted others to experience the same frustrations, but at least she could definitively say it had nothing to do with the accident and murders yesterday.

Instead, she still didn't have answers.

It surprised her when Curtis rested a hand against her upper back. She shocked herself even more when she leaned into it.

Officer Baker gave her a sympathetic look. "I wish I had more answers for you. I'm going to dust the tires for prints and take some pictures. I'll do the same with the window the peeping Tom was messing with. Then, if you'll both come by the police station around two this afternoon, I'll share what we've found out so far. I'm hoping to have a few mugshots to show you, too, just in case you do recognize the man you saw in the woods."

It'd give her time to get her van towed. Then at least she'd be doing something instead of just sitting around. That was definitely preferable.

"That sounds like a plan."

"Good." Baker gave them a nod. "I'll get to it."

The officer got several prints, then he took Rory's as well, so that forensics could rule them out. She'd certainly never touched the tires, and she wasn't sure she'd ever been outside of that window, either. It gave her some hope.

With a wave, Baker got in his patrol car and left.

"It was nice of him to come out here himself," Rory commented.

A lot of things like this were often reported online instead of checked on in person.

"Yeah, it was. You need to call your insurance company and let them know about the tires. They may even recommend a towing company. I'll give you a ride into town."

"Next time, I'm buying." Rory gave Curtis a pointed look and then took another bite of her broccoli beef. This was some of the best Chinese food she'd had in a while.

By the time her van was towed to a local tire store and replacement tires were approved, it was nearly half past noon. Curtis suggested they get some lunch to help pass the time until their appointment at the police department at two.

Instead of allowing her to pay for her own lunch, he'd insisted.

Well, as much as she appreciated the gesture, she couldn't keep letting him pay for her meals, especially since this wasn't a date.

The very thought of being on a date with him was enough to make her cheeks warm. She took a drink of her sweetened iced tea.

"Deal." His eyes twinkled with humor, and she realized that her statement made it sound like she intended to go out to lunch or dinner with him again.

She rolled her eyes to the sound of his deep chuckles.

It was weird. They'd worked together frequently over the last year, yet they almost never ate meals together. Mostly because when they had a break, they were often back at the hospital. She preferred to eat in her van as opposed to the cafeteria, where Curtis often warmed something up. She could count on one hand how many times they'd eaten together, and two of those had been in the last twenty-four hours.

A change in topic was definitely necessary. "I called Karen first thing this morning. She approved my coming back to work like normal after our seventy-two. I did agree to a week-long vacation in July, though." She'd even chosen the dates. Right now, she had no idea what she was going to do with a total of nine days off, but she'd cross that bridge when she came to it.

"That's good. I called her, too. She was a little less enthusiastic, but she said it would be fine for me to return to work on Sunday as well." Curtis finished off a pork egg roll.

He'd ordered three to go with his plate of chow mein and orange chicken.

She nodded toward his arm. "How's it feeling?"

"Not great, but it's not going to keep me from doing my job." He shrugged. "It's not like sitting at home will help it heal faster. What are your plans for the next few days off?"

"I'm going to go into the office at the RV park and see if I can get a better, more well-lit spot closer to the common area. After last night, living at the end of the street doesn't have nearly as much appeal." She wrinkled her nose. She wasn't looking forward to moving everything, but she dreaded the idea of trying not to feel creeped out tonight even more.

"That's a great idea. There seemed to be plenty of empty spots. Surely it shouldn't be hard for them to swap for you. I'm happy to help you move if you need it."

Rory's instinct was to thank him but decline. It wasn't that she avoided help; it was more that she'd gone through most of her life without it.

But Curtis looked so eager, and having someone else there would make things so much easier.

"How are you at backing up a trailer?"

He beamed at her. "I'm your guy."

Ugh. That statement should not mean as much to her as it did. He was simply offering because he was worried about her. Once this case was solved, they could go back to normal.

It was hard because Rory had a great deal of respect for Curtis as a co-worker, but also as a human being. She'd be lying if she said she didn't find him attractive. She'd never considered the possibility of being good friends before— much less more than that.

He had his parents, sisters, nieces, and nephews in his

life. The guy was a dedicated family man who deserved someone who had a much less sketchy family life of her own. Not that he'd be interested in her anyway. She appreciated that he'd gone above and beyond since the accident and shooting yesterday, but she wasn't about to read anything into it that wasn't there.

They finished their food and, since it was nearly two, headed to the police station.

Rory wished she could say she'd never been in one before, but that would be a lie. She'd had to pick her dad up half a dozen times after he'd been arrested for being drunk and disorderly. He never caused destruction of property or hurt other people, which was why he'd been released once he sobered up.

She'd drive him home, and they'd never talk about it again.

"Hey. You okay?"

Curtis held the front door open so she could pass by him and go inside.

Rory realized she'd been clenching her fists. She intentionally relaxed her hands and gave a sharp nod. "I'm good."

They walked up to one of the windows where a woman was waiting for them. "Can I help you?"

"We're here to meet with Officer Baker. We have a two o'clock appointment."

The woman, with Tia written on her name tag, smiled brightly. "You must be Curtis Whitman and Rory Graham. Yes, he's expecting you. If you meet me at the door over here, I'll take you back." With that, she stood and pointed to a door at the far left.

They could see her through the transparent windows as

she walked behind the other counters and opened the door for them.

"Can I get either of you a cup of coffee?"

"That would be great," Rory told her with a smile. "Thank you."

Curtis said he'd like one as well.

Tia led them to a small conference room. "If you'll take a seat in here, I'll let Officer Baker know you're here. And I'll be right back with that coffee."

They chose chairs next to each other on the same side of the table near the end.

Tia returned at the same time Baker walked in. Without a word, she handed out the two cups of coffee, set a variety of sugars and creamers in front of them, and took her leave, closing the conference room door behind her.

Rory fixed her coffee and took a sip. Her eyes widened. "Wow, this is really good."

Baker took the chair on the end and set a stack of files and papers on the table. "I'm not a coffee drinker, but people claim it's some of the best coffee in Destiny. Apparently, Tia gets it from some exotic place and won't let anyone know where."

"Well, it's definitely good." Curtis gave a nod of agreement and set his cup down. "Have there been any new developments in the case?"

The officer's smile faded. "Several, but I'm not sure how many answers we've actually got."

Chapter Eight

Officer Baker arranged everything he brought with him into several piles. The first thing he did was pull two large photos from a manila envelope and put them on the table side-by-side. He slid them over.

"The one on the left is a footprint from the crime scene yesterday. The one on the right is from your place, Rory, on the ground near the window that someone was messing with."

Rory looked from one to the other. Her heart sank as she realized there was no discernible difference between the two.

Curtis put a hand on her shoulder. "They're the same."

"As near as we can tell," Baker confirmed. "Both are a size nine and a half. Our people in forensics did say that this is a common tread, and one of the most common shoes purchased. There's also nothing unique on the tread to confirm they come from the same shoe."

Rory should've taken some comfort from that, but she

couldn't shake the fear that the man who'd shot that couple had been trying to peer inside her trailer. "I'm not a huge believer in coincidences."

Curtis gave her shoulder a gentle squeeze.

"Neither am I." Baker gathered the photos and slid them back into the envelope. "At this point, I think it's safer to assume that both sets of shoe prints were left by the same individual. In which case, I'd again like to encourage you to stay in a hotel or, better yet, with family or friends."

If she allowed herself to think about it now, she'd be way too overwhelmed. She'd figure out her next move once they were done with this meeting. "So, who was the couple?"

"Their names were Greg and Brenda Hoops. They'd been married for four years. No kids. Our medical examiner is conducting autopsies and will give the official reports. Preliminary findings suggest the car sideswiped the tree. It's a late-90s model, so there was a passenger-side airbag, but there were no side airbags. Brenda suffered a bump to the head. Likely from hitting it against the window on impact. It might have been hard enough to cause her to lose consciousness, but our ME believes the cause of death will prove to be the gunshot."

Curtis moved his hand from Rory's shoulder and reached for his cup of coffee, but he didn't take a sip. "And the husband?"

"Greg was found in the woods not far away from the car. There was residue from the airbags, so he was in the car when it struck the tree. He had some bruising on his knuckles and face, suggesting he may have tried to fight against his attacker. The killer shot him three times, which seems excessive. It suggests that either the shooter was trying to gain information from him, or the attack was personal."

Had the killer shot Brenda first and then dragged Greg into the forest? Or had Greg been the first to die? She couldn't imagine how scary their last few moments alive must have been. Rory tried to shut the thoughts out.

She took a drink of her coffee but didn't register the taste. "Do you have any suspects yet?"

"No one concrete yet. I do want to show you a few mugshots just in case we get lucky and you recognize one of them."

"Of course."

Baker handed her a stack of photos. "Take your time."

She nodded absently as she stared at the first face. One by one, she leafed through the eleven photos. Not one of them looked even remotely familiar. She handed them back.

"I'm sorry. I only saw him for a moment. It was as much the way he stared at me as anything." She shivered.

"That's all right. We knew it was a long shot." The officer slid the pictures back into a file folder. "There is one more thing I'd like to show you." He opened his laptop and turned it around to face them.

There was a video pulled up on the screen. It'd been paused.

"Would you be comfortable watching this video for a few moments and see if you recognize this man? I thought video might be more helpful than a photo since we had access to it."

Rory froze. The memory of the man staring at her from the woods made her feel almost sick. What if he were the guy in the video? Was he somewhere in the police station? That thought was more than a little terrifying.

"Look, I don't want you to do anything you aren't comfortable with."

"It's not that. I just didn't expect you to ask something like that. Of course I can watch the video."

Baker waited a moment, probably giving her a chance to change her mind. When she said nothing else, he began the video.

The audio was muted so they couldn't hear what was being said, but she could clearly see the man as he spoke to someone else. When he finally looked in the direction of the camera, Rory shook her head. "That's not him."

"You're sure?"

"Yes. His eyes don't look right. His hair—I think it's too dark. But yeah, I'm sure this isn't the man I saw in the woods. Who is he?"

Baker took back the laptop and closed it. "Greg Hoops' brother, Victor. The brothers own and run a jewelry store in the mall. I feel comfortable telling you this because he was emphatic about talking to a reporter from Channel 2 News after we questioned him this morning. He said the more people who knew the situation, the better because maybe someone would come forward with information leading to his brother and sister-in-law's killer. I imagine the story will be aired this evening if it hasn't already."

The officer didn't look like he approved of the other man's decisions. Rory assumed it was probably because the police liked to keep details close to the vest while they were in the beginning stages of an investigation. Spilling every-thing on the news would not be the preferred way to go about this. She'd seen enough procedural shows to know that much.

"So, what's next?"

"At this point, we're waiting on the ME's official report, and we're going through the Hoops' background, interviewing friends and family, and trying to find something that might lead us to their killer. This wasn't a random act of violence." Officer Baker shuffled some papers together. "In the meantime, be careful. We'll have patrols going by both of your homes as often as possible, but I strongly advise you to be careful. If there's anything out of place, call the station immediately." He stood.

Curtis followed suit. "We appreciate that, and we'll be careful. Thank you for keeping us in the loop."

The men shook hands as Rory got to her feet. She shook Officer Baker's hand as well. "Yes, thank you for updating us on the case. I'm hoping to get my trailer moved closer to the office. I'll make sure to get you that change in space number once I do."

Baker handed them each a business card. "You can even text that information to me directly." He gathered everything he'd brought and escorted them back to the front of the building.

When Curtis and Rory stepped out of the station, she was surprised to see that clouds had moved in and now nearly obscured the sky. "Are we supposed to get more storms today?"

Curtis responded by pulling his phone out and turning on the weather app. He showed her the forecast. "A chance of rain, but no thunderstorms expected until Monday or Tuesday." He pointed to the sun on Saturday. "I hope this is right. My niece's birthday party is supposed to be outside where the kids can run off some energy."

The chance of rain became a reality because they'd barely gotten into his Jeep when large raindrops started to splash the windshield. Curtis turned on the wipers, which created muddy rivulets as the rain washed away the dust that had gathered since the last rain.

At least there was no thunder and lightning to go along with it.

Curtis's voice brought her attention to him.

"Hey. Can I ask you a question? And if you don't want to answer, that's okay, too."

She raised an eyebrow. "This sounds ominous." And serious, if his expression had anything to do with the topic. "What's up?"

He turned slightly in his seat to face her more. "The accident with your mom. Is that why you don't like thunderstorms?"

That wasn't the kind of question Rory anticipated, and it took a moment or two to process her answer. "I was never a fan of them. I think a lot of kids especially are scared of thunder, especially. For me, it was always the lightning. I worried it was going to catch my house on fire. Then the thunder is just like adding insult to injury." She paused, trying to decide how much to say.

Most of this was stuff she'd never told anyone. She'd never had someone she felt comfortable sharing it with. But Curtis was different. Rather than try to rationalize why that was, she continued.

"My parents were usually checked out in one way or another. So when I was a kid, and there was a thunderstorm, I spent it hiding under the covers on my bed or taking shelter in the closet. When we were in the accident, I guess it somehow gave my fear validity. Dumb, I know."

"No, Rory, that's not dumb." He reached for her hand and held it gently in his. "Parents are supposed to reassure us. To teach us that we have nothing to fear from things like that. You never had that in your life." There was no pity in his voice, but there was a tinge of sorrow. "I'm sorry you didn't have that support."

She avoided looking at him directly for fear his kindness, and the emotional weight of sharing something she'd kept buried for so long, might bring unwanted tears. Instead, she stared at their joined hands and tried not to think too hard about how natural it felt.

"Thank you." She took in a deep breath, let it out again, and then thought of something that made her chuckle. "You know, when I chose to move to Texas, I didn't realize how many thunderstorms you guys actually get here. I've always wanted to conquer my fear, but this isn't the way I would've chosen to do it. God certainly has a sense of humor."

"Yes, He does." Curtis smiled then, his expressive brown eyes studying her face. He must've realized they were still holding hands because he cleared his throat and released hers.

Rory ignored her immediate disappointment, which surprised her as much as his holding her hand had in the first place. She clasped hers together and placed them in her lap. He was offering support. Comfort. There was nothing more to it than that.

The silence in the Jeep was weighted. Rory fought for something to talk about, and then her attention landed on the stereo system.

"If the brother was willing to be interviewed this morning, do you think the segment might be available to watch online now?"

"It's possible. For a story like this, I'm willing to bet it was Al Crispin who led the interview. The guy doesn't care what happens or who gets hurt as long as he gets to the story first." His nose wrinkled in disgust. "Al will air it as quickly as possible and hope the facts check out later. Let's see if we can find it."

"I take it you've dealt with him before?"

"A couple of years ago. He doesn't know when to quit." Curtis typed a search on his phone and scrolled through the results. "Ah, here we go. Let's see what the brother had to say."

Chapter Nine

The overweight reporter practically oozed with anticipation as he began the interview with Victor Hoops. Al Crispin was one of those people who gave the impression he'd sell his own mother—maybe even his kid—if it meant getting an exclusive story before one of his competitors got a hold of it.

Curtis had seen him barge onto accident scenes or bother the police for more information when they were still trying to get a situation under control. Any tact or compassion shown was clearly a tool used to further the interview.

It made sense that Victor wanted to find out who was responsible for his brother's murder. Either he was desperate enough to allow Crispin to run with the story, or he didn't realize just how much of a snake the reporter really was.

Curtis held the phone over the console in the middle so that he and Rory could both watch the recorded interview. She leaned a little closer, and some of her hair tickled his arm. He still couldn't believe he'd actually reached for her hand earlier. He'd wanted to comfort her, and that was truly his intention. But once her hand was safely nestled in his, he didn't want to let go.

There was a connection between them, and he was almost certain of it. It'd make things a lot easier if he knew whether she felt it, too.

He stifled a sigh and focused on the interview.

Crispin was standing in a shaded area just outside the police station. "Unfortunately, we have lost two of our citizens in a senseless act of violence." The pictures of Greg and Brenda Hoops briefly came on screen, and the reporter explained that they'd been murdered the previous day. "The Hoops family has been a vital part of Destiny for years. I have Greg's brother, Victor, here with me now."

The camera panned out to show that Crispin was standing beside Victor. "First of all, let me express my sincere condolences for your incredible loss."

"Thank you." Victor slipped his hands into his pockets and then pulled them back out again as though he were nervous.

Maybe he'd been second-guessing the interview.

Crispin moved right along. "I understand this is just one of many losses that your family has suffered in recent years."

"Yes. We lost our father suddenly two years ago to a heart attack. Our mother, who has been suffering from Alzheimer's for several years, got worse once he'd passed. We've since had to put her in a skilled nursing facility to help with her daily life. Through it all, Greg and I relied on each other. Our families have done everything together." Victor's voice caught. "I don't know what life is going to look like going forward."

"I can only imagine what you must be going through."

Crispin paused. "Your father had been a small business owner in our community for many years. Is that right?"

"Yes. He opened Hoops Artisan Jewelry in the mall over twenty-five years ago, and it's still going strong. Or at least Greg and I were trying to carry on in his memory." Victor stopped and seemed to need a moment to gather himself. "I'm not sure how I'm supposed to do this by myself now, but I know it's what our dad would want me to do. I'm thankful I have a wonderful wife and kids to support me."

"That is certainly something to be grateful for. I know I speak for everyone watching when I say that our thoughts are with you, and that we hope the police catch the people responsible."

"Thank you so much."

The camera moved in to frame Crispin's face.

"This is Al Crispin, bringing you the news you care about first."

The video ended, and Curtis turned off his phone before dropping it in the cup holder.

"I don't like that guy." Rory's voice held an edge to it. "He oozes insincerity. But to think of all Victor and his family have gone through... I'll definitely be praying for him and his family."

"Same." When tragedy struck, it was important to have family to be there for you. At least Victor had that. Rory, on the other hand, did not. "How did you make it?"

His question was pretty broad to anyone else who might be listening, but it was clear Rory knew exactly what he was referring to.

"By the grace of God." She shrugged. "There were a lot of times I felt alone and completely powerless. But I always felt His love. I always knew there was something else out there and that eventually, things were going to be better. I didn't know what it would look like, but I clung to that hope. I guess that's what got me through."

"That's admirable. I'm glad you had Him to lean on. Do you have a home church in Destiny?"

"Not yet. Honestly, with our shifting schedules, I guess I just haven't made that enough of a priority. I should, though."

"Next time we have Sunday off, you're welcome to join me at ours. They'd welcome you with open arms." How had he not invited her before now? He mentally berated himself for not thinking of it sooner.

She seemed surprised by the offer. "Maybe I'll do that. Thank you."

"So, what's next on the agenda?"

"You can drop me off at the tire place. I'll wait there for them to finish my van and then head back to the RV park. Talk to the manager about getting my trailer moved to a different spot. I doubt I'll be able to do that today, but hopefully tomorrow."

"Not going to happen."

She blinked at him in confusion. "Which part?"

"Dropping you off. With everything going on, I'd rather not leave you to work on things by yourself. Unless you have a convincing reason otherwise, I was hoping you'd let me tag along today." He prayed she'd say yes. He didn't want to be a stalker, but it'd be hard to drive away knowing she could potentially be in danger.

She looked doubtful.

He nudged her arm with his. "Come on, partner. What do you say? It'll give you a chance to pay me back by buying me dinner later."

That brought a smile to her face, combined with a chuckle. "If you're sure. I wouldn't mind the company."

Four new tires weren't cheap. Curtis didn't miss the way the creases in the corners of Rory's mouth deepened as she pulled out her wallet. She paid the bill and then led the way back to the RV park.

He was surprised to see that many of the empty spots from last night and this morning were now occupied with RVs of various sizes and types. Then he realized it was Friday. Even with rain and storms in the forecast, apparently it was a good weekend to go camping.

Rory parked her van in front of the office, and he pulled into a spot beside it. She didn't need him to go with her, so he waited for her to come back fifteen minutes later. He rolled his window down as she walked up.

"The bluebonnet festival's this weekend."

He'd forgotten all about the annual event held on Saturday at the Destiny fairgrounds. Fields of bluebonnets, a variety of food trucks, plus a large craft show brought in people from all around every year.

"So you can't move right now."

"Not to any of the closer spots." She leaned her arm on the top of his door. "But there is one spot that should be available late tomorrow afternoon. I already told him I wanted it. Space thirty-one." She pointed it out. "Far enough from the restrooms and laundry to not get that traffic going through my space, but close enough to benefit from the extra lighting and being in view of the office."

"That looks perfect."

She nodded. "Yeah, I think it'll work out well. I'll need

to secure a few things in the trailer, but moving it shouldn't be too big of a deal. At least it's a pull-through spot."

Curtis tried to imagine her pulling the trailer all the way from Colorado. By the time she got to Texas, she was probably an expert.

"So what are you going to do about tonight?"

Would she insist on staying in her trailer again after everything that happened last night? Curtis offered a silent prayer that she would heed Officer Baker's suggestion.

Rory chewed on her lower lip for a moment, clearly conflicted. "As much as I hate to do it, I think I'll spring for a hotel room tonight. Assuming I can find a hotel that isn't already full."

"Why don't we go back to your trailer? You can call around, and I'll do what I can to help you get things ready for the move tomorrow."

"I think that sounds like a great plan." She smiled again, and Curtis tried to ignore the way it made his own heart lighter.

At least he wouldn't have to worry about her being here by herself. Surely, with extra people staying at the park, no one would try to hurt her. But he'd much rather they didn't have the opportunity.

Chapter Ten

As soon as Curtis pulled up to the iron gate and punched a code into the security panel, nerves bounced around in Rory's stomach like a bunch of frantic bats. Why did she let him talk her into going to this?

He'd shown up at the hotel first thing this morning, ready to eat breakfast together and go over a plan.

Curtis said he didn't feel comfortable just going to his niece's birthday party and leaving Rory alone for several hours. When she tried to insist that she'd be fine, she could tell he was torn between leaving her and not going to the party. If there was one thing about him that she knew well, it was his devotion to his family.

So when he invited her to join him and insisted that the birthday parties were usually loud with lots of people related and not, she agreed. He seemed thrilled, and at least she wouldn't be sitting around twiddling her thumbs and watching over her shoulder.

But now that they'd arrived at his sister's place, she was beginning to rethink her decision.

Rory wasn't the most extroverted person in the world, and she was going to be walking into a huge family event. It was too late to back out now.

"Now, which sister owns this place?"

"Patty and her husband, Donald. Belle is their oldest, and she's the one who turns seven next week. They also have four-year-old twin boys, Jude and Joshua."

He drove the Jeep through the gate, and it closed behind them. It was a short drive through the trees until they reached a clearing where an impressive two-story brick house towered in front of a circular driveway.

"It's beautiful. The house and the land."

Curtis nodded. "It sure is. I guess Don's always wanted land and horses since he was a kid. It suits their family. It does make for a great party location, too." He chuckled.

"So, real quick. Remind me of everyone's names. I won't remember them, but at least I'll have tried."

He looked over at her and grinned. "You're going to be fine, Rory. I promise."

She fixed him with a serious look.

Curtis ran a hand over his mouth to cover another laugh. He cleared his throat. "My parents are Stanley and Grace. Then my oldest sister is Ashley. She and her husband, Brody, have five kids ranging from the oldest who's twenty down to the youngest who is twelve. Patty is next. Then Kess is only a couple of years older than I am. She and Scott have three young kids with another on the way. I had one more sister, Lisa. She would've been..." He thought a moment. "She would've been thirty-six. She died when she was eighteen."

That last bit of information surprised Rory. She had no idea. "I'm sorry to hear that. It must have been devastating."

"It was. I was twelve at the time. She had a lot of emotional challenges and depression. My parents tried everything to help her, but she eventually took her own life. It was a pretty difficult time for my family then. I only mention her in case someone refers to Lisa, so you know who she was."

He glanced at Rory as though he were afraid it might all be too much information. They bounced over the packed road until they reached the circular driveway. There was a group of kids waiting on the front porch, and all of them were waving frantically.

Rory tried to digest that last bit of information and turned her attention to the kids. "If memory serves me right, you have twelve nieces and nephews if you count the new baby." She tried to imagine what it would be like to grow up with so many siblings or cousins and couldn't even picture it.

"You're good." Curtis rolled down his window and stuck his left hand out to wave back at the kids. "It gets pretty chaotic, but I wouldn't change a thing." He stopped the Jeep and put it in park. "You ready for this?"

"Nope."

That was an understatement. Rory couldn't have been prepared to meet so many new people all at once. Curtis must've given them a heads-up about her joining him because no one seemed surprised. Everyone was kind and welcomed her into the fold as though she'd been coming to these birthday parties for years.

The nerves that had been choking her before faded into the background as they had burgers and chips for lunch and the kids played games.

Kess, especially, made a point of making sure Rory didn't need anything. Curtis had said she was pregnant with their fourth child, but Rory might not have noticed if he hadn't told her ahead of time.

She effortlessly picked up their toddler, Maria, and settled the little girl on her hip.

Rory waved at Maria and chuckled when she grinned and waved back.

"This child doesn't have a shy bone in her body. Do you?" Kess tickled her daughter and gave her a kiss on the cheek.

The girl's laughter was contagious, and Rory was soon joining her. "Sounds like she and her Uncle Curtis have that in common."

"Oh, isn't that the truth?"

Maria squirmed to get out of her mother's arms. Kess set her down and watched as she ran off to join her cousins, where one of the older girls gave her a ride on her back.

It all looked like so much fun.

"I'm sorry to hear about everything you've been going through recently. I hope the police solve the case soon." Kess glanced at Rory. There was nothing but warmth and kindness in her eyes. "I'm glad you decided to come today."

"Thank you. I'm glad I did, too. I have to admit, I was a bit reluctant. As an only child with no cousins, I was worried this would all be a little overwhelming."

"And it isn't?" Kess sounded surprised.

"Oh, it's totally overwhelming. But in a good way." Rory laughed as they watched Curtis wrestle with several of the younger boys. She knew his arm had to be sore because of his injury, but you'd never know by the way he acted. "Curtis clearly loves being a fun uncle."

"The kids all adore him. He'll make an amazing dad someday. You'd think having all of these grandkids around would keep our parents busy enough. But they still like to tease him about having a family of his own soon. Carrying on the family name and all." Kess gave Rory a knowing look, one that she wasn't sure how to interpret.

"So, what do you do when you're not wrangling kiddos?"

Kess shook her head. "Well, I'm a stay-at-home mom, so there's never really a time I'm not wrangling. But we own a section of land out near Lake Buchanan on the edge of town. We've got some cabins that we rent out, and then we own a store out there where we sell camping supplies and things like that. My husband also leads a lot of chartered fishing trips. The kids and I frequently check on the cabins to make sure they're clean and don't need repairs or things like that."

"That's really neat. I haven't been out to the lake yet, but I should do that this summer."

The kids played for a while until it was time to open gifts. Belle seemed to like the wooden Minecraft sign Rory found for her at a craft store. She was glad Curtis had suggested the theme.

Speaking of which, he made a point of routinely checking on Rory to make sure she was comfortable and doing okay. More than once, she found him watching her and giving her a wink when he caught her eye.

By the time they got to the cake, some of the younger children were getting tired. Little Maria had found her mama again and fallen asleep in her arms before she'd even had any dessert.

Kess shifted the toddler and groaned. "I swear, Maria's gotten heavier since I hit the second trimester."

"Do you want me to hold her so you can have some cake?"

Kess seemed surprised by the offer but didn't hesitate. "If you're sure. That would be amazing."

Rory reached for the toddler, who didn't make a fuss as she settled into Rory's arms.

"Thank you. I think I'm going to go use the restroom first and then get that cake. I'll be right back."

"Of course. We'll be right here." Rory sat down in a lawn chair and lightly rubbed Maria's back as she slept. Had her own mother done this for her when she was a baby? Rory would have liked to think so.

All she knew was that, if she were ever blessed with a child of her own, she planned to hold him or her like this as often as she could.

"It looks like you and Kess are getting along well." Curtis claimed a lawn chair near Rory's.

"She's really nice. Actually, your whole family is."

"You sound surprised." He seemed overly pleased with himself. "Told you that you had nothing to worry about."

"Well, I'm happy you were right." Maria gave a little sigh in her sleep that made Rory's heart nearly burst. "It looks like Belle's had a fun birthday. She even came and thanked me for the sign. Very polite."

"Patty's big on being a good hostess." Curtis looked at his watch. "We'd probably better get out of here soon so we'll have enough time to get your trailer moved before it gets dark."

"Yeah, we probably should." She almost hated to leave. "Let's give Kess a chance to enjoy her cake, then we'll leave."

"Sounds like a plan."

Twenty minutes later, Rory was thanking Patty for her hospitality when her phone rang. She thought about ignoring the call, but when she glanced at the number, Destiny Police Department flashed on the screen.

"I'm so sorry. I need to get this." She turned the screen to Curtis so he could see who it was from and then moved away from the crowd so she could hear better.

"Hello?"

"Rory? This is Officer Baker. I just heard an alert over the radio. A fire has been reported at the RV park where you're staying, and it sounds like it might be your trailer."

Chapter Eleven

When Curtis saw that Officer Baker was calling, he'd hoped they might be getting some good news about the case. He knew something was wrong the minute Rory's expression morphed from curious to shocked.

He excused himself from saying goodbye to his dad, who knew the basics about the case, and strode to Rory's side. "What is it?"

Rory ended the call and slipped her phone into her pocket. "My trailer might be on fire." There was no emotion in her voice, which concerned him as much as the news did.

"Stay right here. One sec." He jogged back to his dad and told him briefly what was going on. "I need to get her back to the park. Please apologize to anyone I didn't get to say goodbye to."

"Of course. Keep us updated, and we'll be praying."

"I appreciate that." He spoke the words over his shoulder as he returned to Rory. "Come on. Let's get over there."

Neither of them spoke until they were back in the Jeep. As soon as Rory had her seat belt on, Curtis was pushing the speed limit to get them back as quickly as possible. "What exactly did Baker say?"

"That there was a fire at the RV park and that it sounded like it might be my trailer. He said the fire department was on the way, and he was heading over, too, just in case." She ran her hands through her hair before leaning her head back with a heavy groan. "What am I going to do if it *is* mine?"

"We'll cross that bridge if or when we come to it."

"Right. It might not even be my place." She brought her left hand down to the arm rest and gripped it. "Or maybe it's a dumpster fire or a campfire that's gotten a little out of hand. There are a lot of possibilities, right?"

"Exactly." He reached for her hand again, and this time he held it in his. "Everything is going to be okay."

All of the above was true, but he had a feeling in his gut that her trailer was involved. Judging from the tension radiating from Rory's grip on his hand, he suspected she felt the same. Unfortunately, their fears were confirmed when they pulled into the park and followed the flashing lights.

Rory's trailer was a smoldering black heap that was barely recognizable. Two firefighters manned a hose that continued to douse it with water, causing steam to billow into the air. Thankfully, her van appeared to be untouched by the flames.

Curtis pulled up beside a police cruiser. Officer Baker was standing nearby and approached them as soon as the Jeep stopped. He opened the passenger door for Rory.

"I'm so sorry. I was hoping we'd get here and find there was no fire at all."

"Yeah. Me, too." She got out and shut the door.

Curtis walked around the front of the Jeep to join them. "Who called it in?"

"One of the other campers." Baker motioned to a woman who was talking to another police officer. "We're questioning her, along with anyone else who was here at the time it started. We may not know the cause until we speak with the fire department."

"I can't believe this is happening." Rory's voice sounded wooden. Resigned. "Nearly everything I owned was in there..."

Curtis instinctively put an arm around her shoulders, and she leaned into him. He tried to think of the things he used every day that she might have to replace. Clothing and toiletries, of course. Bedding. Phone chargers. Food. Movies or music collected through the years. And that was all excluding anything personal that could never be replaced, like photos or keepsakes.

His heart ached for what she'd lost.

And yet, if this had happened at night while she was inside, the loss could've been so much greater.

Thank you for keeping her safe, Father. But she's going to need Your encouragement now. Please fill her with peace.

The three of them watched in silence as the fire department finished putting out the fire and started to roll up the hoses and gather their gear.

One firefighter took her helmet off and put it in the truck before approaching them. Her dark red hair had been gathered into a long ponytail at the base of her neck, strands escaping the band after being coiled up underneath the helmet. Granger was the name on her jacket.

Baker took a step forward. "Leslie."

"Hey, Clint." She gave him a nod, her gaze lingering on

him a moment before she turned her attention to Rory. "Are you Aurora Graham?"

"Yes, but you can call me Rory. That's my trailer. Do you have any idea how the fire started?"

"I actually need to ask *you* a few questions first. Are you okay with that, or do you need some time?"

Rory took a step forward away from Curtis and crossed her arms in front of her chest. "Now's fine. The sooner we can get some answers, the better."

"Perfect. I'm Leslie Granger. We tried everything we could to put the fire out, but by the time we'd arrived, it was completely engulfed. There wasn't much to save at that point." She looked to the trailer, then back at Rory. "Do you ever leave anything plugged in and running like a curling iron, blow dryer, or something similar?"

"No. I don't even own a curling iron. I only plug the blow dryer in when I use it, then I unplug it right away. I didn't use it today, regardless."

"What about candles or anything like that?"

"The only candle I have is the one sitting on the picnic table. There's no real counter space inside for one."

Curtis recognized the candle as citronella, the kind that repelled bugs like flies and mosquitoes.

Leslie gave a short nod, clearly filing the information away. "Do you smoke?"

"No." Rory shifted her weight from one foot to the other and dropped her arms. "Unless there was a short in the electricity or one of the outlets, I can't imagine what inside the trailer would've caused the fire."

Baker stepped forward. "We've got an ongoing case involving a double homicide, and one of our suspects may be targeting Rory. If there's a chance this is arson, we need to know about it as soon as possible."

"I get it." She jabbed a thumb at the trailer. "We'll take a preliminary look around and see if the point of ignition is obvious. Either way, we'll get the fire inspector involved. You'll need an official report for your insurance claims. I'll let you know what we find shortly."

"Thank you." Rory took a breath and slowly released it.

"Did you have insurance on it?"

The question came from Baker.

"Yes, thank the Lord." She rubbed her forehead with her right hand. "They're going to love this after claiming the tires on the van. At least it looks like it wasn't damaged. That's something, right?"

Curtis admired her determination to stay positive even after everything she'd been through. "It's definitely a blessing."

Another officer approached, and Baker made the introductions.

"This is Rory Graham, the owner of the trailer, and Curtis Whitman. Guys, this is Officer Josh Carrington."

Officer Carrington tipped his head. "I'm sorry to meet you both under these circumstances. Ma'am, I'm real sorry for the loss of your property."

"I appreciate that."

With a nod, he continued. "I interviewed the woman who called 9-1-1 as well as a few other people who were present. The fire was first noticed around 2:20 p.m. and was called in immediately. No one noticed any suspicious activity around your place, although the park is much busier today with the Bluebonnet Festival going on. According to multiple witnesses, the flames first appeared near the back of the trailer, but it was only a matter of minutes before the entire structure became fully involved."

It was barely noticeable, but Curtis felt Rory's shoulder fall a little.

"Let's get a copy of any security footage the main office might have," Baker told him. "If nothing else, we'll have a record of vehicles going in and out. We may need the comparison in the future."

"You got it." Officer Carrington focused on Rory. "My wife, Penny, volunteers at the Destiny Church of the Nazarene. They keep a supply of personal items for situations just like this." He pulled a business card out of his pocket, wrote a number on the back, and handed it to her. "Please consider calling. They'll get you set up with clothing and all the essentials while you're getting everything figured out. It's not meant to be a charity but rather a blessing they like to pass on to others in need."

Rory studied the number and then gave the officer a smile. "I appreciate that. I'll give them a call once all of this is done."

"I'm glad to hear that." Officer Carrington said his good-byes and then jogged in the direction of the main office.

Rory slipped the business card into her back pocket. "There's one thing I've learned about Texas since I moved here: The people, in general, are really kind. Especially here in Destiny."

"I couldn't agree more." It was one of the many reasons he loved this town and the people in it. He couldn't imagine living anywhere else.

They sat at another picnic table nearby and watched as firefighters examined the remains of her trailer. Curtis found it particularly interesting and hoped that, by this time next year, he'd be a part of the Destiny Fire Department. It was something he needed to talk to Rory about, and soon. He'd sure miss working with her regularly, though.

By the time Leslie Granger came back over, Baker was the only police officer still on the scene. They stood as she approached.

"Like I'd mentioned before, a fire inspector will be by to go through everything with a fine-toothed comb and write up an official report." Leslie reached back with both hands and tightened her ponytail. "That said, there is clear evidence that an accelerant was used. We found the melted remains of a gas can positioned beneath your trailer in the back, along with a lighter. This was definitely arson."

Chapter Twelve

Someone had intentionally set fire to her trailer and destroyed it. But why? If the person who killed the Hoops was afraid Rory was going to identify him if she saw him again, why not try to kill her, too? This seemed unnecessary. Risky.

Whatever the motive, it now meant that, aside from her van, Rory had nothing.

She wasn't about to start living in her van, but she didn't have the kind of money she'd need for a down payment if she wanted to buy a house.

That left renting. She was truly hoping to skip that and go to owning a home once she'd saved enough money. But at this point, it looked like the best option. It would take time to find something, which meant she'd need to figure out what to do in the meantime.

Not to mention replacing some of her necessities.

Rory's head ached trying to process it all.

"Hey."

Curtis's voice, along with a touch to her arm, made Rory jump.

"You okay?"

Officer Baker was watching her, too, and he was clearly concerned.

"I'm sorry. Yes, I'm fine. Well, not fine. But you know, okay, considering." She shook her head. "What did I miss?"

Baker motioned to her trailer. "There was no one who saw anyone lurking around your trailer or messing with it. I'd like to think someone traipsing through the park with a red gas can would at least earn a first look, if not a second one. Which means he must have come from the woods behind the trailer."

Rory looked to the scraggly tree line. It wasn't exactly a forest, but it'd be easy to stay hidden from view if that's what you were trying to do.

If she hadn't already decided to move her trailer, this certainly would've pushed that decision.

Except now that didn't matter.

"If the arsonist did use the trees for cover and come in on foot, then he could've parked anywhere." Curtis frowned.

"True. I'm going to have our K9 unit come down and take a look. Maybe Officer Harrison and Loki can pick up the scent. It's certainly worth a try. Excuse me a moment, please." Baker stepped away to make a phone call.

"You know," Rory began, "when I first chose this spot, I thought I'd lucked out because it felt pretty and secluded like a woodsy getaway. Now it feels vulnerable. Like there could be someone or something lurking just out of sight."

She cupped her left elbow with her right hand and shook her head. She just wished they could get some solid answers.

Baker came back over. "Okay, Harrison's on the way. Look, Rory, there's no need for you to stand around here.

Go take care of some things, I know there's got to be a lot to deal with. I promise I'll call with any updates."

Rory was going to argue that she ought to stay until the investigation had been finished, but another look at her trailer changed her mind.

"That's a good idea. Thank you for everything you're doing."

"Of course."

She turned to Curtis. "I think I'm going to go sit in my van and call my insurance company. Then probably the number Officer Carrington gave me." She also needed a good cry, but that was going to have to wait until later.

Rory didn't realize Curtis had paid for their dinner until it was too late. She glared at him as he walked back to their table, a look of satisfaction on his smug face.

"I thought I was supposed to spring for the next meal," she accused. "Not cool."

"I figured you'd been through enough today. Don't worry, I'll hold you to your promise next time." He stuffed the receipt into his back pocket and sat down again.

He'd asked her to choose anywhere she wanted to eat, and she'd immediately picked The Corner Café. There was something about a big bacon cheeseburger and fries that sounded comforting. The chocolate milkshake definitely didn't hurt.

"Well, thank you. This was exactly what I needed."

"I'm glad."

It'd been a busy rest of the afternoon and evening. Rory reported the fire to her insurance company and got information about what all they'd need to process the claim. After that, she arranged to pick up a box of clothing and essentials from the church Officer Carrington had recommended. Not only did she receive several outfits, but she even got to pick them out.

After that was a stop at the grocery store for some essentials that hadn't been available at the church, like Tylenol, snacks, and anything else she might need in the interim.

Now it was nearly seven o'clock, and it was time to find a hotel for the night. Tomorrow, she'd start looking for an apartment. A task that would've been a lot easier if she had her laptop—which had also been burned to a crisp in the trailer.

She crumpled her napkin and tossed it into the basket that held her meal earlier. When she looked up, she found Curtis watching her with a sheepish look on his face.

"What did you do?"

His phone rang, and he held up a finger as he answered it. "Hey. Yep, she's right here. One sec." He pulled the phone away from his ear and covered the receiver. "My sister, Kess, wants to talk to you."

Rory's eyes narrowed as she took the device from him and put it up to her ear. "Hello?"

"Hi, Rory. It's Kess. I wanted to say how much I enjoyed meeting you earlier today. It was fun getting to visit."

"I enjoyed it, too." And she did, but Rory had a feeling that wasn't all this call was about.

"Curtis told me what happened to your place. Girl, I'm so sorry to hear that. I can only imagine how devastating it must have been. Do you remember my mentioning the cabins we have out near the lake? We haven't rented them yet this spring because they all needed a fresh coat of paint and a few updates, which were finally finished up yesterday." She paused. "Look, I know you need a temporary place to stay, and it's hard for me to believe the timing is just a coincidence. I'd love it if you'd stay in one of the cabins. Each one has a security alarm, there's plenty of lighting, and they're all equipped with wi-fi."

Rory threw Curtis an accusatory look. At least the guy had the decency to look embarrassed—the tips of his ears turning red. "I couldn't possibly do that. I don't know how long it'll be until I find an apartment, and I don't want to keep you from renting the place out."

"We planned extra time to get the updates done. I don't have reservations for any of the cabins until this weekend. You'd be doing me a favor if you stayed in one until then. I can give you a list of the updates, and you can let me know if anything isn't working as it should be."

Kess sounded hopeful. She also seemed on top of things at the party. Rory had no doubt that she and her husband had checked out each and every update to make sure it was done to their specifications. They didn't need Rory to do the same, although she appreciated the effort to make her feel as though she were helping them instead of the other way around.

"How much would it cost through Friday?"

"Let's go with two hundred. But you'll need to check out by noon on Friday." There was a hint of humor in Kess's voice. She was only charging because she probably realized Rory was going to turn it down if she'd offered the cabin for free.

Smart woman.

Either that, or she'd gotten a heads-up from a certain brother of hers. If Rory were a betting woman, she'd go with the latter.

Two hundred dollars was way cheaper than any hotel

she could find. And while being away from town made her a little nervous, the idea of having a security system made up for it.

"That sounds perfect, Kess. Thank you."

"You're welcome. Come by any time, and we'll get you set up. Okay, hand me back to my brother."

Rory chuckled and passed the phone to Curtis.

He listened for a few seconds before responding. "Yeah, I'll show her where it is." He looked at his watch. "We'll meet you there in an hour. Uh, huh. Love you, too."

She crossed her arms and laid them across the table. "You knew I was more likely to agree if Kess offered the use of the cabin herself, didn't you?"

Curtis only shrugged his shoulders, but that arrogant grin on his face said it all. "You may as well know that I decided a change of scenery might be nice. I'm renting the cabin across from yours for the week."

Rory's mouth opened, but she didn't know what to say and snapped it shut again. She wasn't sure if she was more annoyed or touched by his announcement. "That's not necessary."

"Maybe not. I'm sure you're going to be perfectly safe and comfortable there. But what kind of brother would I be if I didn't help my dear, sweet sister by making sure that cabin is ready for her guests on Friday night?"

As much as she wanted to argue against it, knowing she wouldn't be out there alone made her feel better. She prayed that the police tracked down the people responsible for the murders and the arson. If they struck again, the last thing she wanted was for Curtis to get hurt in the crossfire.

Chapter Thirteen

Curtis expected way more pushback from Rory. Of course, if it hadn't been Kess who'd invited her to stay in the cabin, that's exactly what he would've seen. Thankfully, Rory accepted the offer. He wasn't sure what she thought about him staying nearby, though.

It didn't really matter. He wouldn't be able to rest knowing she was out in the cabin alone, even with the security system in place. He planned to talk to Officer Baker, too, and see about a regular patrol. Anything to make these guys think twice about trying to go after Rory again.

After they left the café, she followed him to his house, where Curtis packed some clothes, toiletries, his laptop, and a few other things he thought he might need.

From there, he led the way to Lake Buchanan and the campground and cabins that his sister and brother-in-law had set up. It felt like they were way out in the country, and yet it wasn't quite ten minutes away from the hustle and bustle of Destiny. The perfect combination, and the location was part of why it was doing so well.

Curtis checked his rearview mirror to make sure Rory's van was still behind him and continued the drive. Kess was already there waiting for them. She waved as they pulled to a stop.

She gave him a hug and then turned to give Rory one as well. "I'm so glad you're here. Come on. Let me show you the cabin. We just put new sealant on the exterior..."

He trailed behind the ladies as Kess led a tour of the two bedroom, one bathroom cabin. The living room was nice and spacious, complete with a television, comfortable furniture, and a fireplace. That was Curtis's favorite feature of the cabins. Well, that and the small kitchen in the corner that included a fridge and microwave. It really was like a small apartment, and way better than any hotel Rory might have found.

Kess pointed out the updates they'd made and chatted about some of the others she hoped to do soon. Then she led them to the security system panel.

"All right, here's how you set it when you're ready to stay in for the night." She gave Rory a slip of paper with the code on it and explained how it all worked. "New codes are generated after each guest checks out. If you do accidentally open the door without turning off the system, you'll have about thirty seconds to put the number in. After that, it'll alert us at the main house."

"I'll do my very best not to let that happen." Rory chuckled and tucked the code into her pocket.

"I like people to feel safe, but the security system is as much so, I know that no one's messing with the cabin when it's not occupied. We've had a few false alarms in the past. One year, a storm came through, and hail busted out a window. Another time, someone forgot to latch the door. No need to name names."

Kess batted her eyes and formed a circle with her hands that she held over her head like a halo.

They all laughed.

Curtis put an arm around her. "Yes, my sister, the angel."

"As long as you recognize the truth, little brother." She gave his waist a squeeze. "Is there anything else you need, Rory?"

"I don't think so. Seriously, this place is amazing. Thank you for everything."

"You're welcome." Kess handed Curtis the code to his cabin and a set of keys. "I'll get out of your hair. Call if anything comes up. Oh, and we put a few things in the pantry and fridge for each of you. Have a good night, and get some well-earned rest." She gave them each another hug, waved, and left. The sound of her tires on the gravel road faded as she drove away.

Curtis followed Rory to the kitchen area. She opened the fridge to reveal milk, eggs, orange juice, and a variety of fruits and vegetables as well as butter and condiments. The pantry contained items ranging from bread to cans of soup.

Kess had definitely gone above and beyond.

He'd also talked to her beforehand. If the alarm ever did go off and alert them at the main house, she promised to call Curtis immediately. If there was trouble, he wanted to get a jump on it.

"Your sister is amazing." Rory crossed her arms and leaned against the small counter. "$200 probably doesn't even cover the food. I knew I should've insisted on paying more than that."

"She wouldn't have let you. Trust me, I know." He chuckled. "It's almost nine, and I'm sure you're exhausted. I can get out of here and let you relax for a bit. We'll be getting up and going to work in the morning. Speaking of which, did you want to ride in together or take separate vehicles?"

"Let's take our own. That way, if insurance calls and wants to meet me out at the trailer or something else comes up, one of us isn't stuck waiting for the other."

"That sounds good." Not that he'd let her face any of that on her own, but there was no reason to tell her that now. They'd decided on a time to head back to town in the morning when Curtis's phone chimed with an incoming text.

It was from Officer Baker. Curtis read it aloud.

> The K9 unit tracked the arsonist from the trailer into the woods and eventually to a spot where a vehicle was waiting. Tire tracks, but no video.

"So that's that. At least we know he hadn't just waltzed through the trailer park." It didn't look like that made Rory feel much better. He couldn't blame her. It seemed like the case was full of dead ends.

"I think what we all need is some rest. I'll be leaving the front porch light on all night. You should do the same. Oh! Hold on, I have something in my Jeep for you. I'll be right back."

When he'd grabbed his computer, he'd stuffed his iPad into the backpack as well. When he returned, he worked to set her up a guest log in and connected it to the WiFi in the cabin. "Feel free to borrow my iPad this week. It'll make it easier to look around for an apartment or anything else you need to do online."

He handed it over to her, and his fingers brushed

against hers. He was certainly aware of the connection, and if the way she paused was any indication, so was she.

Rory's cheeks turned pink as she tucked the iPad under one arm. "How did you know I was missing my computer? This is great, thank you."

He shrugged. "I know I would be going crazy without mine. It's no problem at all."

A silence settled between them. It wasn't uncomfortable, but it seemed neither of them knew quite how to break it.

Finally, Curtis cleared his throat. "I should let you get some rest. We've got more storms coming in for the next few days. Work tomorrow's probably going to be busy." He turned to leave, but before he got far, her voice stopped him.

"Curtis?" She waited for him to face her again. "Thanks for staying in the other cabin. I...I feel a lot better knowing you're close by."

Rory was looking up at him now, her beautiful eyes focused on his face.

His hands itched to reach out and see if her hair was as soft as it looked. Then she pulled the corner of her lower lip in between her teeth.

In that moment, he wanted nothing more than to lean in and see what it'd be like to kiss her. To hold her in his arms where he knew she was protected and safe.

With a single finger, he tucked some of her hair behind her ear. As he did, he felt the ridge of the scar she'd shown him before. A scar that spoke of the unthinkable challenges she'd survived. "You, Aurora Graham, are one of the bravest people I've ever known. You're beautiful inside and out, and I'm blessed to know you."

The corners of her mouth lifted, and that's where he placed a gentle kiss. He breathed in the subtle scent of her skin—vanilla with a little spice. When she didn't move away, and instead reached her free hand to rest against his chest, he slowly covered her lips with his own. Rory leaned into him, and he hooked one arm around her waist to steady them both.

He kept their kiss brief even though he could've gone on kissing her forever. If she were as surprised by this as he was, they both needed a minute or two to catch up. The last thing he wanted was for her to regret it in any way.

"I'm really going to leave so you can get some rest."

They both chuckled.

Her palm was still pressed against his chest when he gave it a squeeze. "I'll see you in the morning. Until then, I'm only a phone call away."

Rory nodded at him, her smile shy. "Good night, Curtis."

"Good night."

She walked with him to the door. Once outside, he waited to hear the deadbolt slide into place before he crossed the wide, gravel roadway to his cabin.

He barely got inside before he sent her a text.

> Make sure you set the security system.

> Already done.

Three dots danced at the bottom of the screen, letting him know she was typing something else. They stopped. A few moments later, they were back again. He grinned at the words that popped up.

> Don't forget, I'm buying lunch tomorrow.

Before all of this happened, they normally ate lunch on their own. The fact that she automatically assumed they'd be eating together was a good sign.

I'll hold you to it. Sleep well.

You, too.

Chapter Fourteen

Last night felt like an eternity. It didn't help that Rory started out feeling spooked when she got cleaned up before bed. There was something about being alone in a strange place and vulnerable in the shower that freaked her out. She kept listening for the sound of the security system alarm while she took one of the fastest showers known to man.

Once she got out and dressed, she made sure the alarm was still on and then went through the cabin room by room to verify that she was the only one there. It was one of the few times in her life that she'd wished she carried a gun.

By that time, the adrenaline surges guaranteed that it'd be impossible to go to sleep. She grabbed an apple and the iPad Curtis let her borrow, and took them to the couch in the living space.

Rory had every intention of trying to look for apartments, but whenever she tried to focus on something, her mind went back to that amazing kiss. There'd been a few times in the last day or two when she'd wondered if he might be thinking of her as more than just a colleague. She'd hoped he might eventually see her as a friend, especially after spending so much time together lately.

She had *not* seen that kiss coming. It was a good thing he'd put his arm around her. Otherwise, she might have ended up a puddle on the floor.

Would it be weird when she saw him in the morning? Would it make working together awkward? Surely not, but she couldn't help worrying about it. At the same time, that kiss made her desperately want another.

Maybe that was why it was so frustrating to not sleep well all night. Sure, she could've dreamed about that kiss. Goodness knows she wouldn't have minded reliving it a time or two.

Instead, she kept dreaming about people sneaking around outside the cabin windows or dousing it in gasoline and starting a fire.

The nightmares woke her up frequently. It wasn't until four in the morning when she finally fell asleep and didn't so much as move until her alarm went off at six-thirty. She sat groggily on the edge of the bed for a moment, but she couldn't give herself too long. She only had an hour before she and Curtis had to leave for the hospital.

It took longer to get ready in a strange place, plus having to open new containers of deodorant, socks, and other essentials. She grabbed a banana and finished it just in time to walk out the door at seven-thirty.

Curtis was already locking the door to his cabin when she stepped onto her porch.

They met where their cars were parked side-by-side.

"Good morning." He greeted her with a smile that held a hint of something different between them. "Did you have a good night?"

"I've had worse."

His eyes narrowed a little as he looked at her. "But you've had better."

She shrugged and resisted the temptation to touch her face. Hopefully, her eyes weren't too puffy and there weren't dark circles under them. "What about you?"

"Same. Drive through for coffee on the way?"

"Absolutely."

There was a heartbeat of awkward silence before he reached over and placed a hand on her shoulder. "You lead the way. I'll be right behind you."

A giant cup of her favorite coffee was the pick-me-up she needed. Once at the hospital, they checked in with Karen and then went right to work. While they didn't get a call out right away, Rory was tasked with showing the new EMT, Jessica, how to go through their two waiting ambulances and check all the medical kits to make sure all necessary supplies were stocked and ready for the next emergency.

It was one of the first things she learned to do when she was hired at the hospital. In fact, it was Curtis who showed her where everything was.

Speaking of... she hadn't seen him since they first got there. Several people who worked the ER called in sick, and Curtis was sent down to help with triage until more people came in.

Jessica seemed nice, and Rory truly didn't mind showing her the ropes and getting to know her, but she was looking forward to seeing Curtis at lunch.

Dark clouds rolled in as they finished going through the inventory for the second ambulance. The weather app on her phone said there was a chance of thunderstorms today and tomorrow. She'd been hoping it was wrong.

"So, how long have you been living in Destiny, Jessica? Are you used to these thunderstorms?"

Jessica looked out the window and nodded. "I've only been here for a couple of years, but I've lived in Texas most of my adult life. I'm used to them. You?"

Rory told her about moving from Colorado a year ago and how she was still trying not to worry about tornadoes every time a big storm moved through.

The first clap of thunder sounded in the distance.

She looked at her watch. "Looks like it's about time for lunch. I don't know about you, but I'm starving."

Jessica patted her stomach. "Same. I think I'm going to drive home and let my dogs out before it starts raining. See you in a while."

"Yep, see ya." Rory texted Curtis to let him know she was heading to the cafeteria.

He was already there waiting for her when she arrived.

"What'd you do? Run as soon as you got my text?" She chuckled.

"No, I speed-walked, and I was closer to the cafeteria than you were." He winked. "They've got barbecue today. Let's get a plate before they run out."

Hospital food, in general, had a pretty bad reputation, but Destiny Community Hospital served some mean Texas barbecue a few times a month. Rory's mouth watered just thinking about the tender brisket, savory sausage, and crisp okra. She made sure to pay for both of their meals and earned a wink from Curtis in the process.

She'd already popped several pieces of okra in her mouth by the time they claimed a table. Both were silent for a while as they ate. Partly because the food was so good and partly due to the ambient noise.

A particularly large group of people finished eating and left, bringing the noise level down substantially.

Curtis wiped his hands off on his napkin. "Did everything go okay this morning?"

"Yeah, it was fine. Jessica and I cleaned and restocked two of the rigs. Nothing too exciting, which after the last few days, isn't a bad thing. How about you?"

"ER was a mess. They were super short-staffed this morning, but seem to be back to normal now. I guess that means you'll be stuck with me for the rest of the day." His eyes twinkled as he tried to hold back a smile.

"Sounds horrible." She didn't even try to fight her grin. "I think we've got a transport—"

Thunder boomed, making Rory jump. A moment later, the rain began to pelt the windows that lined one wall of the cafeteria. Lightning flashed in the darkened sky outside.

"We'd better get back." Curtis stood and gathered their plates. "The call-outs will be starting soon."

"Yep."

It was a grueling shift filled with multiple trips into the weather and helping the hospital transport patients to different floors and wings. The evening meal was a protein bar eaten on the road. With only thirty more minutes left in their shift, the rain was finally tapering off with a promise of similar weather tomorrow.

Rory finished mopping the floor of the rig. It took a second pass to get all the mud up, but it was finally clean again. Curtis had been working on the exterior, hosing off the brown coating from all the puddles they'd driven through.

When she exited the ambulance, she looked up at the sky. It was an odd combination of dark clouds giving way to lighter ones with patches of blue peeking out between them.

Texas weather could be so dramatic sometimes.

By the time she and Curtis were walking out to their vehicles, Rory was struggling to keep the yawns at bay. *Please, God, let me get some sleep tonight.* She wasn't sure she could take another restless night like the last one.

Curtis nudged her arm with his. "You going to be able to drive back to the cabin okay?"

"I'll make it. I'm not sure what I'm looking forward to more when we get there—sitting down, eating something, or just getting some sleep."

"I'm with you." They stopped at her car, and he reached for her hand. "It was weird because we spent the majority of the day together, but there wasn't really a chance to talk. I wanted to make sure you were okay with what happened last night."

He studied her face. It was starting to get dark, and the remaining clouds in the sky were beginning to show hues of orange and yellow. It cast a strange light on everything around them.

"Yeah. I'm good." Rory felt suddenly shy as her cheeks warmed. "Really good. I'm just not sure what it's going to mean when it comes to work. I don't want things to change if Karen decides we need to work separately."

"That's something I was hoping to talk to you about..."

A breeze blew through the parking lot, catching something on the window of her van. They both noticed it and turned to find a large piece of paper taped to the glass.

"I thought they'd put a stop to local restaurants leaving flyers on people's cars." Rory reached for it and carefully peeled it off the window. "Leaving a flyer does not make me want to eat at..." she opened the paper so she could see the name of the restaurant and froze.

"Rory? What is it?"

Numb, she held the note out so he could read it.

Written in block letters, it said,

YOUR TIME IS RUNNING OUT.

Chapter Fifteen

Rory accepted the cup of coffee with a thankful nod of her head. Unlike the last time she'd visited the Destiny Police Department, the office wasn't nearly as busy since it was technically after business hours. Of course, officers were always on duty, and apparently, Officer Baker had been working late.

She'd been surprised when, after Curtis sent Baker a text to let him know about the note, they were asked to bring it by the station. Baker met them at the main door himself to let them in.

He'd taken pictures of the note and then carried it down to forensics.

"We already know your fingerprints are going to be on the paper, but maybe our suspect got careless, and his will be, too."

Rory had her doubts. Maybe there'd be something about the paper—something special—that would lead the police to the person who bought it. It was always so nice when that happened on detective shows. With her luck, it'd probably be a piece of copy paper that was common in just about every office building in town.

"Where do you park your vehicle while you're working?"

The question came from Baker and pulled Rory's attention back to the room.

"Out in the parking lot behind the hospital."

"So it was out in the open."

"Yes." Rory looked from Baker to Curtis. "Why do you ask?"

"Because the paper was completely dry, and there was no warping like there would be if it'd been wet at some point and then dried out later." Baker pulled up the photo he'd taken of the note and turned it around to show them.

Curtis, who had been sitting in one of the chairs at the conference table, got to his feet and crossed his arms. "It was raining until an hour before we left work."

"Which means the person who left this either waited until it was dry to tape it to the window, or knew what time you got off work and wanted to make sure it didn't get too wet or blow away." Baker started walking to the conference room door. "I'll be right back. I'm going to have footage pulled from the hospital's security system. We've got a narrow window of time. With any luck, it'll have caught something."

Rory took another sip of her coffee but barely noticed the taste. "What if he was out there watching us walk back to our cars?"

The very thought scared her more than she liked to admit. There'd been a part of her that had hoped, after burning her trailer, that would be all she'd have to deal with. That whoever was responsible would move on to some other obsession.

Curtis said nothing. Instead, he moved to stand behind her chair and put his hands on her shoulders. "They're going to find him. We're not going to let anything happen to you."

He kissed the top of her head, and she allowed herself to soak in the reassurance he offered.

"All right," Baker said as he re-entered the room. "I've got someone working on that now. While I've got you both here, I have a few recent developments in the case."

He motioned for Curtis to sit down and then grabbed a seat himself.

Curtis took the one next to Rory. "Was the ME able to get any more information from the autopsies?"

"Yes. The woman in the car, Brenda Hoops, did suffer some minor injuries when the car impacted the tree. All those injuries were prior to being shot. The gunshot wound was the official cause of death, and it was likely instantaneous. There was no reason why she couldn't have gotten herself out of the vehicle, so the fact that she was still wearing her seat belt suggests she was shot and killed soon after the accident occurred."

Possibly in front of her husband. Rory tried not to think about that. She didn't want to imagine what they might have gone through...

Curtis reached over and took Rory's hand. He ran the pad of his thumb back and forth across the side of her finger. "How about the husband?"

"He had defensive wounds on his hands, and contusions suggest he was struck multiple times. The gunshots were the cause of death. We were able to dig a slug out of the victims' vehicle. You were right. The shots came from a .38. Ballistics confirmed that the same gun was used to shoot both victims and at the two of you."

Rory closed her eyes and pictured the man staring at her and how, even while she was watching him, someone had taken a shot at them. "That means, while there were likely two people there, only one was the shooter." It didn't necessarily make her feel better. It just made her even more confident that the man she'd seen was not the one who'd pulled the trigger.

Curtis nodded. "Maybe one man dragged Greg into the woods while the other shot his wife."

"It's possible. I assume you both saw the interview with his brother, Victor, on the news?" When they said they had, Baker continued. "We checked into his story, and it seems to be true. His father died just as he said. His mother is living in an assisted living facility here in Destiny. I called over there to see if I could question Mrs. Hoops, but the nurse I spoke with said she's rarely lucid."

It was all so horribly sad. For all intents and purposes, Victor had lost his entire family. Rory was thankful he still had his wife and kids to lean on. "Have you found any reason the Hoops were targeted in the first place?"

"Not yet. We've done a deep dive into their financials. There were no red flags. Neither of them had a record outside of a few speeding tickets between them. They had the usual debt like cars and a mortgage, but no secret offshore bank accounts. Regular payments went to the facility where his mother is being cared for. There wasn't a whole lot left in their account by the end of each month, so it could be they were struggling a little financially. On paper, they were a completely normal couple."

Curtis leaned back in his chair, a frown on his face. "What about the brother? Did you look into Victor?"

"He told us he was at the jewelry store at the mall when the Hoops were killed. His phone and car GPS both place him there at the time of the murders. There are cameras in the jewelry store, but there are none in the office, which is where Victor reportedly worked. The cameras show him coming into the building but not leaving. His alibi seems to check out."

Rory stifled another yawn. Because of the way Greg Hoops was killed, Baker had mentioned that it led them to think he knew at least one of the shooters. Or, at the very least, it wasn't a random act of violence. Which meant there had to be a tie to the murderer out there somewhere. "So what's the next step?"

"At this point, with no real leads, I'm sure Detective Walker is going to start looking into the jewelry store itself. Apparently, the wife was really into yoga, so I'll go down and speak with people at the studio she frequented. See if she said anything to anyone there." He put his hands on the table and pushed himself to stand. "I think we should all go home and get some rest. I'll call you guys tomorrow and let you know what we find on the note."

"That sounds good." Curtis stood and reached a hand down to help Rory do the same. "We appreciate everything you guys are doing."

"Not a problem at all. You guys stay safe. I've got a patrol going through the campground and cabin area regularly all night long. If anything comes up, don't hesitate to call."

Baker took them back to the entrance, they all shook hands, and then Rory walked with Curtis back to their vehicles.

She couldn't help but eye her van as they approached. The tires weren't flat, and there were no suspicious papers taped to any of the windows. She unlocked the door and opened it, which triggered the internal light to come on.

Glances through the windows assured her that no one was inside waiting.

When she turned to Curtis, she expected him to be amused or even ready to tease her. Instead, he was watching her with approval.

"Have you considered getting your License to Carry? Have you ever been shooting before?"

"I've never even held a gun. To be honest, I'd never really considered one until the last few days. Now? Yeah, I'm considering it." Her own father would've hated the idea. He'd always been vocal about his dislike of people carrying weapons larger than a Swiss Army knife.

"There are classes here in town that you can take. We'll do some research and find one for you once all of this is over." Curtis helped her into her van. "For now, let's get back to the cabins. Stick close, okay?"

Rory was glad to follow Curtis. Now that it was dark, she wasn't sure she would've found her way back to the cabins on her own. A sense of relief washed over her as they pulled up to them. She'd intentionally left all the lights on inside. The combination of that plus the porch lights casting a warm glow made her cabin feel welcoming.

All she needed was a shower and some sleep.

Immediately, she remembered the fear that had nearly choked her last night while trying to shower and the nightmares that had plagued her all night long.

She just wanted to go home. Except, she didn't have one.

Suddenly tired and completely overwhelmed, she crossed her arms over the steering wheel and rested her forehead against them. "God, please give me strength." She breathed in. Out.

A tapping on her window brought her chin up to find Curtis peering through in concern. "Are you okay?"

Rory released her seat belt and got out of her van.

He must have read something in her eyes because he didn't hesitate to pull her into a hug. She rested her cheek against his chest and focused on the steady sound of his heart. With each beat, her worries eased a tiny bit.

"We've got this," he reassured her as he lightly rubbed her back.

There was something about his use of the word *we* that filled Rory's chest with warmth. Here, in his arms, she felt safe. The realization that she'd felt that way only a handful of times in her life brought tears to her eyes. She took a steady breath and blinked them away.

"Thank you." She barely heard her own words, so she wasn't sure that Curtis had heard them at all until he tightened his hug and rested his chin on the top of her head.

"Of course."

"Can I ask you for a ginormous favor?"

He leaned back, his arms still loosely around her waist, and raised an eyebrow. "I'm going to say yes, because I'd do just about anything you asked me, with the caveat that I can change my mind if you want me to rob a bank."

That made Rory chuckle. "Deal." She swallowed and searched for the right words, because now that she was about to voice it out loud, she felt a little silly. "Would you come inside for a half hour or so? Last night, being here alone...I freaked myself out, I guess. I kept listening for the alarm to go off while I was in the shower, and then it was like that all night long. I know, it's ridiculous—"

"No, it's not. I don't blame you one bit. I'll just bring my computer over and check my e-mail and things like that while you get cleaned up."

"Really? You're sure you don't mind?"

"Not even a little." He paused. "I'm not trying to make you uncomfortable, but if you want, I can stay here in the other room tonight. Or sleep on the couch. If you think it'll help you get some rest."

The very thought of not being in the cabin alone pushed a heavy weight from her shoulders, and it suddenly felt as though she could breathe easier. Her eyes teared up again. Stress and lack of sleep were not a girl's friend. "As long as you're not uncomfortable with the idea yourself."

"Truthfully? I didn't sleep well, either. I kept getting up and looking over here to make sure no one was messing with your cabin. I think we'll both rest better if we're in the same place. I just need to go get some things quick, and then we'll be set."

"That sounds perfect." She leaned forward and let her forehead rest against his chest a moment. "Thank you."

"Hey." He waited for her to look up, then ran the backs of his fingers down her cheek. "I've been thinking about our kiss all day. Would it be okay if I kissed you again?"

Rory rocked forward onto her toes. "Yes, please."

With a smile, he kissed her softly. Slowly. And for those moments, it made her forget the danger that seemed to be lurking just around the corner.

Chapter Sixteen

Getting a decent night's sleep made all the difference in the world. Even though Curtis woke up two different times and checked to make sure everything was fine, he went back to sleep easily. He never heard Rory so much as stir until her alarm went off at six-thirty in the morning. When she came out of her room, dressed and ready for the day, she looked more rested and seemed to be feeling less stressed.

They made scrambled eggs and toast for breakfast, decided to share his Jeep for the commute to work instead of driving separately, and stopped for coffee along the way.

At a red light, he took in her olive-green blouse that brought out the copper in her hair and eyes perfectly. Pairing that with black jeans created an outfit that was hard to ignore. "You look beautiful today."

Rory's cheeks flushed as she smiled shyly. "Thank you."

He reached for her hand and gave it a squeeze. He could easily get used to this. Tonight, once their shift was over, he would tell her about going through training to be a paramedic with the fire department.

Curtis was a little nervous because he didn't want to do anything to disappoint her. However, it would remove any issues that their boss might bring up when it came to working together as a couple. Assuming she was open to that. Because he very much hoped that was the direction this was going.

He needed to talk to her about that, too.

"We're supposed to get more storms over the next few days." Rory's voice betrayed her disapproval. "It seems like a lot. Is this what most springs look like here?"

"We do get a lot of rain and plenty of storms, but the severity has been worse than normal this year. All the water has been great for our lakes and streams, though." He released her hand so he could turn into the hospital parking lot.

"Very true. I guess I'd rather have storms in the spring and hope the extra rain means fewer wildfires this summer."

"Exactly."

They were about to get out when Curtis's phone rang, Officer Baker's name popping up on the screen.

Curtis swiped to answer and put it on speaker.

"Hey, Baker. I've got the phone on speaker, and I'm here with Rory."

"Perfect. I'll just keep you both a moment. There were no fingerprints left on the note that was taped to your window, Rory, except for yours. I don't think any of us are surprised by that, though. Video footage of the parking lot wasn't much more helpful. It showed someone putting the sign on your van, but he wore a black jacket with the hood pulled up over his head. No logos and no view of his face."

Curtis wasn't surprised, but he was disappointed that they didn't find something more helpful.

Baker continued, "Detective Walker did find out that the jewelry store Greg and Victor ran had some major issues with a disgruntled customer. Apparently, he stormed in and insisted that the gold watch he'd purchased for a relative was fake. The watch he tried to return was supposedly not the same watch he'd purchased, and he threatened to come back and make them pay him what they owed him."

"Wow. Sounds like it got pretty heated." Curtis exchanged a look with Rory. Maybe this would lead to some progress in the case. Her eyes lit up with hope.

"We're trying to track the customer down so we can question him, but I do have a picture of him from the surveillance footage that Victor Hoops handed over. I'm texting it now. Rory, please let me know if he looks familiar to you."

"Sure." They waited for the ping. Curtis opened the photo and turned it toward Rory.

"I'm certain this isn't the guy. I've never seen him before." She slumped against her seat in disappointment.

"Well, if we're right and there was more than one person in those woods, we can't rule out this being the guy you didn't see. We'll locate him and bring him in for questioning. If anything else comes up today, I'll reach out."

"We appreciate it."

They ended the call.

Rory wrinkled her nose. "I was really hoping that was going to be it."

"I know. Me, too."

Curtis put the rig in gear. "Ready to head back?"

Rory fastened her seat belt and nodded. "Let's do it."

They'd just finished transferring an elderly gentleman from Destiny Community Hospital to one of the best in-patient rehabilitation centers in the area. Their temporary patient, Mr. Nash, was an absolute hoot. By the time they got him there and moved into the facility, Curtis felt like he'd known the man for years. If Mr. Nash's humor and positive outlook on life were any indication, he'd recover from his surgery and be back home with his wife before he knew it.

A wife that, as far as Curtis could tell, their patient loved fiercely. Even when he joked about a fight they had or something she'd said, it was abundantly clear that he adored her and missed her terribly. And no wonder. According to Mr. Nash, they'd been married for over forty years—relationship goals, right there.

For now, he and Rory would return to the hospital and work there until they and the ambulance were needed again. Unfortunately, storms were rolling in with heavy rain, hail, and potential tornado activity predicted. The number of car accidents could potentially skyrocket. They weren't likely to be at the hospital for long.

They'd barely traveled two blocks when the dispatcher came over the radio.

"Unit one, report to the Destiny Mall. There's been an accident in the parking lot involving a car and a pedestrian. The pedestrian is a woman in her forties who may have a broken leg. A police unit is already on the scene."

Rory reached for the radio just as lightning flashed across the dark sky. Thunder wasn't far behind. She grimaced.

"This is unit one. We're responding with an ETA of five minutes."

"Understood."

Rory returned the radio. "We're practically around the corner from the mall. If the woman was hit by a car, she's lucky if all she's got is a broken leg."

"You're not wrong." They'd need to check for signs of head or internal injuries. It was impossible to know what kind of condition the accident victim would be in until they got there. They didn't even know how fast the vehicle was going when it struck her.

Even though the speed limit should be slower in the parking lot, that didn't mean drivers always followed the recommendation. Then you had pedestrians who didn't pay attention when they walked to or from their vehicles.

Whatever happened, it wasn't their job to figure out who was at fault. They'd arrive, take care of their patient to the best of their abilities, and leave it to the police to sort out the how.

They got a more specific location from dispatch as they turned into the main entrance to the mall. It wasn't hard to spot the accident. A police car was already there, red and blue lights flashing, and there was quite a crowd that had gathered. Thankfully, they cleared out of the way to allow Curtis to maneuver the ambulance as close to the area as possible.

He recognized Officer Baker standing between a woman lying on the ground and a man who was clearly agitated. Both individuals appeared to be yelling at each other. As soon as Curtis opened his door, their angry words floated across the thick and humid air.

He and Rory got their medical gear and headed that

way. More lightning and thunder had her casting a furtive look toward the sky.

"The pedestrian always has the right of way, and there aren't exactly crosswalks zigzagging through the parking lot." The woman lying on the ground had propped herself up on her right arm and was jabbing her left pointer finger at the man. "You were driving like a maniac."

"You weren't paying attention to anything but your cell phone. You walked right out from behind that van and were still looking at the screen when you hit my car." The muscles in the man's neck were tight with anger. He scratched a bald spot on the top of his head and took two steps forward.

"*I* hit *your* car?" The woman's voice rose in pitch as she started to push herself up to sit. Her sandy blonde hair, which had some debris in it, was a mess of tangles framing her face. A strong wind blew through and only matted her hair further.

Officer Baker put out a hand to stop her. His nearly six-foot frame helped when it came to taking command of a tense situation. A firm, deep voice didn't hurt, either. "Ma'am, you need to stay still until your injuries have been evaluated." He turned to the driver. "Mr. Copeland, if you'll move to the side over there. I can take your statement, and the paramedics can do their jobs."

The man started to object but did move away. Baker motioned Curtis and Rory over. "I'm surprised to see the two of you here. I was coming in to talk to someone at the jewelry store when the accident happened. I didn't see it, but I was obviously the closest one to respond."

Rory nodded. "We were maybe five minutes away and got diverted for the same reason."

Baker tilted his head toward the woman. "Mr. Copeland seems to think she's faking her injuries."

"We'll check her out."

The officer went to work getting the other guy's statement. At least he'd managed to establish a decent perimeter, allowing them room to work without too much of an audience.

Curtis knelt beside the woman. "Hello. My name is Curtis Whitman. Can you tell me who you are?"

"Kristy." It took several seconds for her to quit glaring at the driver and turn her focus to Curtis. "My right leg hurts. A lot."

"All right, Kristy. This is my partner, Rory. We're going to look at your leg. Are you injured anywhere else?"

"Some scrapes from the pavement." Kristy rotated her left arm to show them the damaged skin on her elbow, wrist, and palm.

The wounds didn't look serious, although they'd need to be cleaned and bandaged.

Rory placed an oximeter on Kristy's finger. "Did you hit your head at any point?"

"No. The bumper of his car hit my leg, and then I fell. At least I caught myself." She held up her scraped palm again for emphasis.

While Rory took their patient's vitals, Curtis checked on her leg. The skin wasn't broken, but a large bruise was already beginning to form, and it was clear Kristy was in a great deal of pain. Given the location, there could be a hairline fracture.

"We need to transport you to the hospital where the doctors can get some X-rays. It's important that we see what's going on with your leg before you try to put weight on it."

He gave Rory a nod, and she stood and jogged to the ambulance. The wind, which had only increased in persistence in the last few minutes, tossed her hair around. She pulled it together at the base of her neck and shoved it down the back of her shirt, but that didn't last more than a moment or two.

Another flash of lightning was followed closely by more thunder. Almost immediately, several large raindrops fell on the pavement nearby. One hit the exposed skin of Curtis's neck near the hairline, and the surprisingly cold water sent a shiver down his back.

Rory returned with a brace, and they worked together to secure it around Kristy's leg to stabilize it for transport.

By the time they'd finished, a torrent of rain had begun to fall. The combination of cold water and the wind made every raindrop sting the moment it hit bare skin. The onlookers who had stuck around were hurrying toward shelter. The sound of the rain hitting the pavement, vehicles, and the metal roof of the mall nearly drowned out the crackle of Officer Baker's radio.

Curtis was about to go back to the ambulance for the stretcher when Baker and Mr. Copeland, the driver involved in the accident, ran toward them.

Baker pointed toward the mall. "A tornado warning has just been issued. We need to get inside!"

Curtis glanced upward at the dark, angry clouds that had an almost green tint to them. That was never a good sign. As if on cue, the tornado siren in the distance cut through the wind.

The metallic pings on the mall roof announced the arrival of hail mixed in with the rain. The wind swept through the parking lot like a turbulent wave.

Together, Curtis and Rory helped Kristy to a standing position then pivoted with her between them. There was no time to get the stretcher from the ambulance. The five of them made their way past several vehicles and across the parking lot to one of the main mall entrances. The tall trees in the courtyard outside offered some protection from the sting of the hail.

Inside, the same warning was being issued over the loudspeaker in the mall.

"Please make your way quickly and calmly to the tornado shelters located on each end of the mall near the restrooms."

People who'd been watching the rain from the glass doors and windows turned to follow directions.

Before they could get far, a crack was immediately followed by a deafening roar. Curtis looked back just in time to see one of the large trees in front of the mall entrance crash through the glass doors.

Acting on instinct, he stepped around Kristy to stand behind both her and Rory, using his body to block any flying debris from hitting them.

Shards of glass skittered all over the tiled floor. Pieces hit the back of his jacket and landed in his hair.

All around them, people screamed. Someone screamed and fell to the floor on his right.

Officer Baker's voice rose just above the din. "Everyone to the storm shelter!"

With that, he helped the fallen woman get up and guided people forward.

The man who'd hit Kristy with his car appeared, put an arm around her waist, and helped her along.

Curtis refused to look behind them to see if the

increasing wind and hail were heralding a tornado. Instead, he kept Rory in view and tried his best to keep people moving, all the while praying that everyone would make it to the shelter safely.

Chapter Seventeen

Rory tried not to think about the possibility of a tornado tearing apart the front of the mall. That very fear had nearly rooted her in place moments before until Curtis had pressed a hand to her back and urged her forward. Instead of thinking about the what ifs, she made herself focus on the people around them. She helped an elderly man who struggled to move forward with his walker.

The group reached the hallway where the restrooms were located and followed the signs to the tornado shelter near the end. There were already people inside, and Officer Baker jogged forward to stop the door from closing. He motioned for everyone to move past him into the room.

Rory knew about tornado shelters, but she'd never been in one. She'd imagined it would either look like a root cellar or some fancy high-end panic room.

This was definitely closer to a root cellar. It reminded her of a small warehouse with chairs lining two of the walls and cabinets built into another. More chairs were stacked in one corner. People were already sitting while others got more chairs down and were distributing them around the room.

Mr. Copeland made sure to bring one over for Kristy and eased her onto it so she could get off her wounded leg, then dragged a chair over and insisted that she rest her foot on it before getting another for himself.

"Are you okay?" Curtis put his hands on Rory's shoulders. "Were you hurt?"

Nothing hurt, and a quick inspection didn't reveal any obvious cuts from the glass. "No. I'm fine. What about you?"

"Maybe a couple scratches if anything at all."

Thunder boomed, and Rory jumped. "I hate this." She crossed her arms tightly in front of her to ward away the chill settling in. Likely a combination of nerves and her rain-soaked uniform.

The lights flickered and went out, plunging them all into darkness. Less than thirty seconds later, they came back on, just not as bright.

Curtis pulled her into a hug. "The storm knocked out the power, but it looks like they have generators going to the shelters. We're okay. We're safe in here. We just have to wait out the storm." He pulled back and gently cupped her face in his hands. "We need to keep it together. There may be some people who have been hurt. Focus on them. On the job."

"Yeah." She could do that.

Curtis's hair, which was normally perfectly in place, had been tousled in the wind. The sight made her smile despite everything they'd just been through. She reached up and raked it back in place with her fingers. "There, that's better."

He pinned her with an amused look before lowering his hands and moving into the crowd.

Rory straightened her back and scanned the room which seemed to be getting more packed by the second. Several children cried as their parents reassured them. The chairs were all occupied, and people were either sitting or lounging on the floor.

A man's voice rose above the din. "How long are we going to have to stay in here?"

His question seemed to encourage others

"Was the mall hit by a tornado?"

"What if it rips the roof off?"

A young child cried harder.

Officer Baker's jaw tightened. "Bringing everyone here is out of an abundance of caution. As soon as the storm clears and the *potential* danger has passed, we'll all be able to get back to what we were doing."

A little boy, around eight years of age, walked up to Rory and pointed to the first aid kit that she still had with her.

"Do you have any Band-Aids?"

Thankful for something to focus on, Rory shifted her bag around and held it with both hands. "I sure do. Do you need one?"

The boy shook his head. "It's for my little sister."

Rory raised her chin to find Curtis watching her, approval in his eyes.

He turned to the crowd. "Has anyone else been injured?"

She offered the young boy a comforting smile. "Why don't you take me to your sister, and we'll see what we can do?"

He led her through the crowd of people to one wall where a man sat on a chair with a little red-headed girl on his lap. She had her face buried in his chest as she cried. The father rubbed her back while he held a handkerchief to her arm.

"Dad! This lady has a Band-Aid for Nora."

Rory knelt before the man and his daughter and set her bag on the floor. She gave the duo a smile. "I sure do. Nora, did you hurt your arm?"

The little girl, who Rory guessed to be around four years old, nodded and sniffed, but she kept her face against her father's chest.

The man carefully removed the handkerchief. "She was cut by some glass when the doors and windows shattered."

Rory suspected Nora wasn't the only one who'd received a similar injury.

She zeroed in on the wound. No wonder the child was crying, the glass had left a long cut. Thankfully, it didn't look very deep. She opened her bag and pulled on some gloves.

"Nora, I'm going to take a closer look at your arm, okay? I just want to help you feel better."

The little girl nodded and turned her head just enough to peek at Rory. The father continued to soothe her with words of encouragement.

Rory knelt on the ground and took some supplies out of her bag, setting them on her knee. "I'm going to use some butterfly bandages to close the cut and then bandage it." When the father nodded his agreement, Rory got to work cleaning the wound. "Honestly, if the cut were on her face, I'd recommend you take her to the doctor after this is all over and have it closed with stitches. You're more than welcome to do that if you want to. But the butterfly bandages should be sufficient, otherwise."

The man looked down at his trembling daughter and shook his head. "I think she may have had enough excitement for one day. Thank you for taking care of her."

"You're welcome." Rory smiled at him, then finished closing and bandaging the wound. "There we are, Nora. Good as new. How does that feel?"

The girl finally leaned away from her dad, looked at her arm, and then offered Rory the smallest smile.

Rory collected the trash and turned to look for Curtis. He was wrapping an elderly woman's knee. He spoke calmly to the woman and helped her with confidence. The woman gave him a kind smile.

His ability to get people around him to relax and trust him was one of the many things Rory admired about him.

Thunder from outside was loud enough to rattle the walls. Several people cringed, and that included Rory.

She hadn't been through this bad of a storm before. At least not like this. Would they be released from the storm shelter as soon as the immediate danger had passed? Or would they stay until the storm itself was over?

Rory's thoughts drifted to the stormy night her mom had insisted they leave their home. Dad had been so angry, and his raised voice would stick with her long after he disappeared from the rearview mirror. As a child, she'd blamed herself. Wondered if there might have been something she could've done to stop the argument.

She'd planned to talk to her mom and try to convince her to go back. She never got that chance. If only it hadn't been storming. If only her mom had waited until the next day to leave.

But none of it was in her control. Just like today and, really, the last *few* days.

Thank goodness she knew Someone who *was* in

control. "Father, please protect everyone here. Keep us safe, and help the storm to lose power so that no one else is in danger."

She'd barely ended the whispered prayer when the door to their packed storm shelter banged open, and a man strode in. Officer Baker immediately moved to speak with him, only to turn and head toward Curtis a moment later.

Rory made her way through the crowd in time to hear Baker explain the situation. "There's an older gentleman who fell near the food court. Other emergency crews should be on the way, but he's in a lot of pain."

Curtis turned his focus to Rory. "If you'll finish this, I'll evaluate the situation."

"Of course. Be careful, huh?"

"You, too. I'll be back as soon as possible."

Rory nodded and watched him long enough to see that he left with the man who'd come in earlier.

With a reassuring smile, she finished wrapping the woman's knee and then spent the next twenty minutes or so patching cuts and scrapes and stabilizing a sprained wrist. She sent up a silent prayer of thanks that no one had been hurt more seriously.

Curtis was right. Staying busy was the best way to keep her mind occupied. She hoped everything was going well for him and his patient.

The door to the storm shelter opened again, and Officer Baker came back in. He had his arm wrapped around a pregnant woman who was wet and shivering.

"Rory? There should be some more blankets in one of the back cabinets. Could you grab one for me?"

"You've got it."

The first cabinet only yielded bottles of water and a nice sized first aid kit. She moved to the next one and quickly pulled on the door. A half-dozen blankets were folded on one of the shelves. She snatched two and pushed the door shut again.

Rory was about to turn away when something pulled her attention to the left, where people were sitting on chairs on the other side of the cabinet. Her gaze scanned the faces of those waiting out the storm but stalled when she saw a man wearing a baseball cap. His chin nearly touched his chest as he stared at his feet.

And then he raised his head, and the air rushed from her lungs.

The man looking back at her was the same man she'd seen in the woods.

Chapter Eighteen

Even if Rory had doubted her own memory, it was clear by the way the man's eyes narrowed that he recognized her, too. The hair on the back of her neck stood on end as a sensation like ice water slowly flowed down her spine.

His gaze flicked past her to the other side of the storm shelter and then back again. Was he feeling cornered? Or was he daring her to make the first move?

There wasn't a thing she could do, so she tucked the blankets under her arm and turned, forcing herself to walk toward Officer Baker with a confidence she certainly didn't feel. Halfway there, she heard a rush of footsteps. Before she could turn, the man shoved her aside and ran past her to the door of the shelter.

Rory stumbled over someone else's feet and barely stayed upright. The commotion had gotten Baker's attention, but the suspect had already slipped out of the shelter.

She hurried to Baker and the pregnant woman. "It was the man from the woods. I have no doubt about it. He recognized me, too."

The officer shook out one of the blankets and draped it over the pregnant woman's shoulders, then directed her to a chair. Rory took the other blanket and put it over the woman's lap.

"Description?"

"White. Late thirties." She tried to picture how tall he was as he bumped into her. "Maybe six feet tall. Dark blue eyes. No facial hair. He was wearing a navy-blue T-shirt and a matching baseball hat. I didn't notice if there was anything on the hat."

Baker gave a single nod. "Take care of her. I'll call it in." He started speaking into his radio.

Rory tried to focus on her new patient. "What's your name? How far along are you?"

"Lynn. I...I'm thirty-three weeks." The poor woman's teeth were chattering. Her brown hair hung in wet sections around her face. "I got caught in the storm and had to run around part of the building to get inside."

"I think it caught all of us by surprise. How are you feeling?" She subtly reached for Lynn's wrist and checked her pulse. It was fast but not dangerously so.

"I'm okay. Just really cold." When Rory released her wrist, Lynn rested both hands over her protruding stomach. "I was hoping to do a little baby shopping. Now I'm wishing I'd waited for this weekend when my husband was off work."

The color was returning to Lynn's cheeks. "It'll be a good story to tell your baby. Do you know if it's a girl or a boy?"

Lynn smiled brightly. "A girl. We're naming her Courtney."

"That's a beautiful name. Congratulations."

"Thank you. And thank you for the blankets."

"You're welcome. Just sit tight and get warmed up. As soon as we hear the tornado warning has been lifted, we'll let you all know."

Lynn nodded.

Rory moved to stand beside Baker who looked less than happy. "There are two units headed this way, but there's no one here now. I did let mall security know and asked that they detain anyone who matches that description." He looked doubtful.

"It'd be easy to slip out in all the chaos. Or to ditch the cap and change shirts."

"Exactly. Do you think you could talk with a sketch artist later? See if we can come up with an image?"

"Absolutely." After seeing the man's face twice, Rory didn't think she'd ever be able to forget it. "I'm going to call Curtis. If this guy is out there, Curtis needs to be aware."

"Good plan."

Instead of using her radio and clogging up communications, she tried her phone, but she didn't have a strong enough signal to go through. Most likely because of the storm shelter. Instead, she typed out a text.

> I just spotted the man I saw in the woods. He took off. May still be somewhere in the mall.

She gave him a description of the man, hit send, and prayed it would go through. It seemed to, but she felt better when her phone pinged with a response.

> This man can't be moved. His hip is broken. As soon as he's headed for the hospital, I'll come find you. Please be careful.

I will.

The lights flickered and grew brighter. Apparently, the power was back on.

If being confined bothered Rory before, it was really irritating her now. Judging by the way Officer Baker looked, he was ready to pounce on anything that moved. He was feeling the same way. He spoke to someone on his radio, then stepped into the center of the room.

"Okay, everyone. The tornado warning has been lifted. We've been cleared to leave. However, the west entrance is going to be a mess with glass and debris. You're going to want to go out a different way, even if it means having to walk partway around the mall."

"Did they say whether it was a tornado?"

The question came from one side of the room and was quickly followed by a barrage of others. Rory was wondering the same thing herself.

Officer Baker held up his hands to quiet everyone. "I don't know the answer to that. Given rotation was seen above the mall minutes earlier, I think it's a distinct possibility. It also could have been a downburst. We may not know for sure until the experts have time to go over all the information and review satellite imaging."

The officer turned to face Kristy Norris, who was still sitting down, her splinted leg propped up in front of her.

"I've been told there's another ambulance waiting outside to transport you to the hospital. I'd like to move you to the east entrance. I'll let them know you're coming."

Mr. Copeland, the man whose car had struck Kristy in the first place, stood quickly. "I can help her get there."

He held out a hand, and she took it with a grateful nod.

Baker motioned for Rory to come closer and lowered his

voice. "I'm going to escort them. Once this tornado drama has cleared, they'll likely be at each other's throats again over the accident. I don't want there to be any accusations of further injury. I'll get her onto the ambulance and then assign someone else to take the report. Can you handle things here until I get back? I've got officers who are supposed to head this way as soon as they get to the mall. Everyone is watching for the suspect."

"Yep, I've got this." She shifted to the side as several people walked past, all eager to escape the confines of the storm shelter.

With a nod, Baker turned to Lynn and suggested that she come with them. At the very least, she'd have help getting to the mall exit where she'd texted her husband to pick her up. He helped support Kristy, and the four of them left.

Rory turned to survey the room. Only a handful of the occupants were still inside. Once the last person left, she did, too, and closed the shelter door behind her.

"Nora!" A deep voice called, an edge of desperation to it. "Nora, where are you?"

The little girl's father came around the corner holding his young son's hand. "Have you seen Nora?"

"No. I just checked, and the storm shelter's empty. What happened?"

"One minute, the three of us were leaving the shelter and talking about getting ice cream, and the next, she was gone."

Rory pictured the sweet little girl. The thought that she could be wandering somewhere on her own was a scary one. "There were a lot of people leaving at once. Maybe she followed someone else thinking it was you and didn't realize it until she'd gone far enough to lose sight. Which store is her favorite?"

"She loves the girly store. The one with all the earrings and little trinkets."

One of the security officers came into view, and Rory flagged him down. They told him the situation, and he called it in so that all officers in the area could start looking for her and had an announcement made over the loud-speaker.

Rory prayed they'd find the girl quickly. She turned to the father. "You go check the earring store, and then check the food court in case she went there for ice cream. I'll check the bathrooms and the play area on the other side of the mall." Rory could imagine the little girl needing the restroom after all the excitement. She pulled her phone out. "Let's exchange numbers. If you find her, please call me. And I'll do the same."

"Thank you so much."

They traded numbers. Then father and son ran off with the security officer while calling Nora's name.

With her phone in one hand, Rory jogged to the women's bathroom was just down the hall from the storm shelter. She pushed it open to find several women inside. "Have any of you seen a little girl come in here?"

They said no, but Rory ducked down and looked for little feet beneath the stall doors. "Nora? Are you in here?" Nothing. "If you do see a little red-headed girl, she got separated from her dad. Please let mall security know immediately."

The women in the restroom said they would be watching for her as an announcement went over the loud-speaker giving a description of Nora, asking people to keep a lookout for her.

Rory stepped back out into the hall. Now that the crowd was thinning out, she realized just how long and winding the hallway was. What if Nora had ducked into the bathroom out of desperation, but when she came out again, she turned in the wrong direction? It would certainly be easy to do, especially for a little girl who was probably frantic to find her dad.

"Nora!" She jogged down the hallway away from the main part of the mall, passing a locked janitorial closet and several doors with numbers on them. "Nora! Honey, I'm here to take you to your dad. He's looking everywhere for you."

Further down the hall was an open doorway that led to a break room. Rory flipped on the light, but there was no sign of the girl. She doubted Nora would've gone much farther than this without turning around.

Rory was just about to head back when her phone rang. It was Nora's dad, Joel. "This is Rory."

"Hey, we just found Nora. She was by the ice cream store just like you said. Thank you so much for your help. Now and earlier, when you patched her up. I appreciate it."

She smiled and breathed a sigh of relief. "I'm so happy to hear that. You're welcome. You guys enjoy that well-earned ice cream."

Joel chuckled. "We will."

The call ended, and she slipped the phone back into her pocket.

"Hey! Stop!"

The voice came from the direction of the mall. By the time she registered that it was Curtis's, something crashed into the side of her head, and an intense pain drove her to her knees right before darkness swallowed her whole.

Chapter Nineteen

The moment he made sure his elderly patient was settled in the ambulance, Curtis pulled off his gloves, slipped the strap of his medical bag over his shoulder, and took off at a run for the storm shelter.

Now that the tornado warning had been lifted, people were milling about the mall, most of them talking about the intense weather and wondering whether they'd had any damage at their own homes.

He turned the corner and continued down the hall to the storm shelter to find the door closed. He opened it anyway, but no one was inside.

Two women walked toward him.

"Excuse me. Did you happen to see my partner? She's an EMT and would've been assisting with everyone who had been waiting in this storm shelter."

"She came into the women's restroom a few minutes ago looking for a missing little girl. Maybe she looked further down the hall?"

He'd heard the announcement about the missing child

moments ago. It made sense that Rory was trying to find her.

"Thank you."

An unease he couldn't explain fluttered around in his chest. He pulled his phone out and was just about to dial her number when he thought he heard her voice up ahead.

As Curtis rounded the corner, he spotted Rory with her back to him, talking on her phone. Between him and Rory, a man held a red fire extinguisher over his head.

"Hey! Stop!"

The man reacted, paused for half a second, and then swung the extinguisher at Rory.

To Curtis's horror, her body crumpled to the ground like a rag doll as the man who attacked her dropped the fire extinguisher, jumped over her body, and ran farther down the hallway and around a corner.

"No, no, no!" He landed on his knees beside her and dialed Baker's number. He put it on speaker, then lifted her arm and rested his fingers against her wrist. Her pulse was steady, and he sent up a silent prayer of thanks.

"Baker here."

"Rory was just attacked. We're in the hallway down from the storm shelter near room 209. The suspect ran off in the opposite direction. I have no idea where this hallway leads. I'm rendering aid, but she's going to need to get to the hospital."

"Copy that. I'm on my way."

He hung up and then used his radio to call dispatch. He reported that Rory had been injured, he was there, and they would need transport to an ambulance immediately.

He vaguely noted a report over the loudspeaker announcing that the missing child had been located.

"Rory, can you hear me?"

Curtis turned to look at the fire extinguisher on the ground nearby, and the realization that the blow could've killed her instantly hit him hard. "Please, God, let her be okay."

He leaned over her so he could see where she'd been hit. An ugly bruise was forming on her head above her ear on the left side. There was no bump, but that wasn't necessarily a good thing. Not if it meant there was internal bleeding. He couldn't rule out a skull fracture, either.

Footsteps pounded on the floor behind Curtis. He turned to see Baker approaching.

"I've got officers going around the other side. If this guy's still here, we're going to find him. I never should've left her, but I had to escort someone to an ambulance." His expression looked pained. "Is she going to be okay?"

"I hope so. I'm waiting for someone to come in with a stretcher so we can get her to the hospital. I've got her. Go catch this guy."

Baker nodded once, drew his weapon, and proceeded down the hall and around the corner after Rory's attacker.

A muscle in Curtis's jaw twitched. He understood why the officer might be blaming himself. Curtis was wishing he'd stayed in the shelter instead of leaving, too. The fact was, they all had a job to do, and they knew what they were signing up for. That included Rory. It'd be easy to play the blame game, but it was the person who attacked Rory who needed to pay for what he'd done.

Curtis had every confidence that Baker would have a hand in tracking these guys down, just like he had every intention of making sure Rory would make it out of this okay.

The image of that man trying to bash Rory's head in

had him clenching his fist in anger. If he hadn't come down the hall when he did...

A low moan brought Curtis's attention to Rory's face as she slowly tried to roll her head to the side.

He shifted his weight and placed a hand on each side of her head. "Rory, you need to stay right where you are."

She moaned again and tried to lift her eyelids. He barely saw a sliver of her amber eyes before she squeezed them shut again as though the light were too bright to handle.

"Curtis? Where are we? What happened?" The words were said with some effort.

Curtis tried to ignore his rising concern. Confusion certainly wasn't unusual after a head injury of any kind. Still, he'd feel a whole lot better once they got her to the hospital and ran some tests.

"We're at the mall. We responded to an accident in the parking lot then had to come in to the storm shelter. Do you remember that?"

"Yeah." She groaned again and grimaced. "I was trying to find Nora."

"The missing girl. I heard she's been found."

"Her dad called me to tell me right before..." She opened her eyes a sliver. "What happened? What's wrong with me?"

He might've tried to sugarcoat it for someone else, but Rory was an EMT. The more information she had, the more she'd understand why she needed to be still and stay awake.

"Someone hit you in the head with a fire extinguisher. You're awake and aware, so that's good. But I don't know yet what kind of damage might have been done."

For a moment, she looked like she might doubt what he

said. She raised a hand to touch the injury and hissed with pain. "A fire extinguisher. I might have a skull fracture."

"A concussion at the very least. That's why I need you to stay still until the other EMTs arrive. We'll get you transported to the hospital and see what we're dealing with."

"Right." She closed her eyes again. "I'm freezing."

"It's the adrenaline fading." He wished he had a blanket or coat to give her, but he wasn't about to leave her side. Until the guy who attacked her was caught, there was no guarantee that he wouldn't double back to finish what he started.

Less than a minute later, two EMTs rushed in with a stretcher. Curtis never felt so helpless as he stood by and watched them put a brace on Rory's neck and then carefully lift her onto the stretcher.

He reached out and snagged her hand. "I really wish I were riding with you."

A ghost of a smile tugged at the corners of her mouth. "I know. But you'd better get our rig back, or you'll never hear the end of it from Karen."

He took some comfort in the sound of her voice. At least she was conscious. Talking. "I'm going to be right behind you."

Waiting.

Curtis seriously hated waiting, especially when he wasn't sure of the outcome.

He'd walked with Rory until they'd loaded her into the ambulance, and then he'd retrieved the one they'd driven to the mall and followed them back to the hospital. Doctors were ready for her as soon as she arrived and whisked her away, the doors whooshing shut behind them.

Normally, Curtis was the one who gave a brief overview of the patient's condition, watched them disappear behind those doors, and then went the opposite direction to wait for his next assignment.

This was different. This time, he wanted to go with Rory to make sure she was okay. But even if they had allowed it for family—and they didn't—that still didn't include him.

Instead, he went to the waiting room and immediately called Karen and updated her on what was going on. He and Rory would have all kinds of incident reports to file after this call out.

"Listen, I know she doesn't really have any family. Who is her emergency contact? Should we give that person a call?"

They'd all had to update that information at the beginning of the year, and adding an emergency contact was mandatory.

Karen didn't speak for several seconds, but Curtis could hear the clicking and clacking of a keyboard in the background.

"It's you, Curtis. Didn't she ask you first?"

Karen sounded about as surprised as Curtis felt. To know that Rory had trusted him enough to choose him even before things started to change between them was a big deal.

"Maybe she did, and I don't remember." A lie, and he felt bad about it. But he didn't want Rory to get into any trouble. He certainly would've remembered if she'd asked him to be her emergency contact, even if it'd been back when they first met.

"I'll make sure the department knows to relay her condition to you. Keep me updated."

"Will do." He ended the call and strode over to a nearby nurse's station. "Hi, I'm here with Rory Graham. She was just brought in with a head injury. I'm her emergency contact and would appreciate regular updates on her condition. Karen Beltway should be calling to verify that fact for you shortly."

"I'll update you as soon as I get that call." The nurse gave him a reassuring nod.

"Thank you."

He headed back to his chair but couldn't make himself sit down. Instead, he walked to the row of windows looking out at the parking lot.

The clouds had finally started to clear, and sun beams broke through. Looking out there now, it was hard to believe the violent weather they'd experienced less than two hours earlier.

Except the weather wasn't the only thing that'd been violent.

He pushed away the unwelcome images of Rory being attacked and of seeing her there lying on the ground unconscious.

Curtis sent texts to his family asking them to pray and his church as well. Then he closed his eyes.

"Father God, please be with Rory as the doctors work on her. Give them wisdom to know what to do to help her the most. Please help the police to catch the person who hurt her before he can harm anyone else."

Chapter Twenty

Thunder echoed in the darkness. Great booms that Rory could feel in her bones but weren't accompanied by lightning. It took a moment for her to realize that there was no light at all. Had the power gone out in the storm shelter? Was a tornado about to tear them all apart?

Fear gripped her heart like a vice. The lack of light meant it made no difference whether her eyes were open or not, and yet she squeezed them shut as tightly as she could.

Suddenly, the air shifted around her, and she began to rock back and forth. Rory slowly opened her eyes. Instead of the storm shelter, she was sitting in the passenger seat of a car.

Immediately, she knew where she was. She didn't want to be here. Not again.

Fear and anger swirled around in her belly until she thought she might be sick. She gripped the edge of her seat and refused to look at the driver. She knew who was behind the wheel.

Rain pelted against the windshield as the wipers tried

their best to clear it away. Tall trees whooshed past her window.

"Please slow down. Please slow down." She chanted the words over and over. If anything, the car only picked up speed.

She knew what was next, and she was helpless to stop the chain of events.

A low laugh came from the driver's seat. Rory swung her gaze from the darkened landscape outside to her mother. But instead of the woman she knew so well, a man sat behind the wheel instead. A man with blue eyes and an intense stare that never wavered as they careened off the road and right into a tree.

A sob caught in her throat at the same moment that a hand grasped hers. A strong hand that was much bigger than her own.

"Rory? Everything's going to be okay. You're safe."

The voice sounded familiar, but Rory struggled to identify it. She tried to open her eyes, but the light was so bright that she instantly closed them again. She focused on his deep voice and the way his thumb rubbed across the top of her hand, back and forth in a calming pattern that allowed her to slow her breathing.

This time, when she opened her eyes, she tried to focus. The room around her was so bright that it took several moments to adjust to the difference.

She turned her head—the motion sending pain echoing through her skull—to find Curtis sitting in a chair nearby. He held her hand in his, his brown eyes watching her closely, his forehead creased with concern.

Her gaze skittered around the room.

She was in the hospital. She vaguely remembered being

transported by ambulance after Curtis found her on the floor at the mall.

A sharp pain radiated from the side of her head. She reached her free hand up to touch the spot, the contact only causing more discomfort.

"Please tell me—" Her voice caught, and the words sounded hoarse. She cleared her throat.

Curtis released her hand and reached for a small table nearby to retrieve a plastic cup with a straw. He held the straw to her lips so she could take a sip of cool water. She nodded her thanks, the motion sending more pain through her skull. She flinched.

"What time is it?" She looked around the room for some kind of indication, but with no clock or window, she found none.

She tried to sit up, but the combination of a headache and Curtis's gentle hand against her shoulder stopped her.

"Take it easy. You don't want to rush this. It's almost five in the evening. It's been a few hours since you were brought in. It's good you were able to get some rest. You need as much of that as you can get."

Rory frowned. "They didn't give me any pain medication, did they?"

If there was one thing she'd learned about her parents' struggles with addiction, it was that she had to do everything in her power to make sure she never ended up in a similar situation. Addictions like that could be hereditary.

"Only acetaminophen. With your concussion, they wouldn't want you to have anything stronger anyway." He gently squeezed her hand. "I know you wouldn't want any narcotics. I can't tell you how much I admire you for your decision."

The truth of his words was written on his face, and knowing she had his support meant the world to her.

"So, what's the verdict? What kind of damage are we looking at here?"

Curtis pushed the call button. "The doctor is making his rounds and was hoping you'd be awake when he did."

She nodded, then wished she hadn't. She tried to focus on her surroundings. There was a blood pressure cuff around her upper left arm and an IV taped to her arm. A pulse oximeter hugged her pointer finger on the same hand. A glance at the monitor reassured her that her vitals were normal.

She moved her limbs and took stock of her injuries. The only thing that hurt was her head, but the pain was no joke.

It was only a few minutes before the doctor and a nurse came in.

Rory knew full well that patients usually had to wait hours to see the doctor. She supposed it was one of the perks of working at the hospital. She'd take it.

The nurse began to make notes in her chart.

The doctor, who was older with gray hair, a round face, and bristled eyebrows, shifted his glasses from the bridge of his nose to the top of his head. She'd never met him before, but she'd seen him around a few times.

"It's great to see you awake, Ms. Graham. I'm Dr. Prescott. How are you feeling?"

Rory looked from the doctor to Curtis and back again. "My head hurts. A lot. It's pounding."

Even her eyes ached and begged her to let them close to block out the light.

The doctor performed several tests as he kept her talking. "Tell me the last thing you remember before waking up here."

She swallowed hard and wished she had more water to drink. She almost asked for the cup but changed her mind because what she really needed was answers.

This time, she allowed her eyes to close and tried to focus her mind. She reported a much shorter version of what she'd told Curtis. She knew the doctor was checking to make sure there was no memory loss after the blow to her head. She should be okay there. Or at least, she thought she should. But if she'd forgotten something, would she realize it?

She forced her eyes open again but breathed a sigh of relief when she caught Curtis giving the doctor a nod of agreement.

Nausea coiled in her stomach as the pain in her head intensified. She was vaguely aware of the beeps from the heart rate monitor as they picked up tempo.

"You're doing great," Dr. Prescott assured her as he leaned against the counter by the sink. "You were extremely lucky, young lady. You do have a concussion, but I would classify it as mild. There are no skull fractures or brain bleeds. I have no reason to think you won't make a full recovery."

That was a relief. Rory started to touch the spot on the side of her head again, but stopped herself. Did it look as bad as it felt? She was probably lucky the hit hadn't killed her.

The nurse must have finished getting the information she needed because she left the room.

Dr. Prescott pushed away from the counter and gave her a serious look. "You're going to have to take it easy for a while. Even a minor concussion can leave you with headaches, dizziness, moments of confusion, and even some temporary memory loss. My point is, don't overdo it. Listen to your body, because it's going to tell you when you need to slow down."

Rory was thankful she hadn't been hurt worse. But take it easy and slow down? That wasn't really in her vocabulary. "How long do I need to stay here?"

"I don't see any reason why you can't go home. I would like you to schedule a follow-up with your physician next week. I'll also give you the contact information for a neurologist. It wouldn't hurt to reach out and schedule an appointment. It's better to be proactive about your care and hopefully not need it later." He patted her hand kindly. "In the meantime, the best thing you can do is get some rest."

Dr. Prescott went over the signs to watch out for, reminded her that a repeat head injury could be extremely dangerous, and again insisted that she get as much rest as possible. Since her concussion was mild, she didn't need to be awakened regularly at night, so that was a plus.

He offered a prescription for pain medication, which she turned down. Over-the-counter medication would have to do.

Right now, she just wanted to go home. Being in the hospital brought way too many memories that she'd worked long and hard to bury.

"I promise I'll be careful. Thank you, doctor. I appreciate it."

"You're welcome." He gave her an encouraging smile, Curtis a nod, then left.

Now that it was just her and Curtis, the room seemed so empty. But with the beeping of the machines and all the other hospital noises coming in from the hallway, it was far from quiet.

A chime sounded, and Curtis glanced at his smart watch. "That was Officer Baker asking how you're doing.

They just finished processing the crime scene. I think he's going to want to ask you some questions."

"Will you please tell him that we'll let him know once we're back at the cabin? I just want to get out of here first."

"Of course." He typed a response on his phone.

Rory asked the question she thought she already knew the answer to. "Were they able to catch the guy who did this?"

When Curtis gave a subtle shake of his head, Rory groaned.

A murderer had tried to kill her today, and he was out there somewhere.

Chapter Twenty-One

Unfortunately, saying they were going to release Rory and actually doing so were two different things. Over an hour had passed, and the nurse still hadn't returned with the discharge papers. Rory was getting frustrated, which Curtis totally understood.

When his stomach growled, he realized she was probably hungry, too. He told her he was going to get her something to snack on. Besides, leaving would be the best thing he could do, because more than likely the nurse would be by, and then Rory would be waiting on him instead. At least that's what they were hoping would happen.

Unfortunately, Rory's frown when he returned told Curtis that it didn't happen. At least she was sitting up now, and some color had returned to her face. That was a good sign. "Well, I brought coffee."

She accepted it readily, cupped it with both hands, and breathed in the aroma before taking a sip. The happy little sigh afterward made him smile.

She did that with every cup of coffee he'd seen her drink, and he thought it was adorable—every single time.

"I owe you." She took another sip.

"How about owing me double?" He produced a blueberry muffin with a flourish.

Rory chuckled and accepted the pastry. "Thank you." She set the coffee down on the little rolling table nearby before pinching a piece of muffin off and putting it in her mouth. "I needed this."

Curtis had bought himself the same thing. He settled into the chair and started to eat his own. "Can I ask you a question?"

"Sure." Her eyes narrowed a little as though she were afraid of what he might ask. Apparently, the facial movement made her head hurt because she winced.

"After you arrived at the hospital earlier, I went to speak to Karen. I asked her to look up your emergency contact." He ignored how she looked down at her muffin. "I figured I should call them for you. Let them know what happened." He paused to give her a chance to say something. When she didn't, he asked outright, "Why did you put me down as your emergency contact?"

"Hmmmm." Rory slowly chewed her bite of muffin, then set it down on the small cart. "I didn't have anyone local to list. But once I met you, I may not have known you well, but I knew you were trustworthy." She shrugged. "I figured that was better than making up a name. I never figured anyone would need to call."

"I can appreciate that. I don't mind. I was just curious. I'm glad you did, because it allowed me to get updates on your condition until I could check on you in person."

Rory reached for her coffee, but she didn't take a drink. "Thanks for not being weirded out. Don't worry. I will change it after—"

"Don't."

She looked at him in surprise.

"I don't mind, and you need someone you can count on. I hope you know that'll always be me." He meant it professionally, of course, but it was more than that. He cared for her—a lot—and he wanted to see where this new relationship led. He hoped she did, too.

She dipped her chin. "Thank you."

Rory was about to say something else when the nurse walked into the room with several papers in her hand.

"Sorry it's taken so long. It's been one of those days. I've got your discharge papers here along with the instructions the doctor went over with you." She pulled out an iPad. "If you'll sign here, and here, you'll be free to leave. I'll go grab a wheelchair and be right back." She turned to Curtis. "If you'd like to bring your vehicle up to the ER entrance, I'll bring her down."

He told her he would and stuck his head out into the hall. Nearby, a hospital security officer by the name of Lafferty had been assigned that floor after the attempt on Rory's life. Curtis flagged him down. "They're releasing Rory Graham now and taking her by wheelchair down to the ER exit. I need you to please go with her and not let her out of your sight. I'll meet you there."

"I've got it." Lafferty entered the room and stood to the side to wait.

Curtis reached for Rory's hand. "I'll see you in a few minutes."

Officer Baker was already waiting at the cabins by the time Curtis and Rory drove up. Curtis had been in contact with the officer by phone and had given Kess a heads up so she knew what was going on. After everything Rory had been through today, it was kind of Baker to offer to come to the cabin to ask her questions so she could sit down and put her feet up.

Rory had remained silent for the drive from the hospital with her head resting against the window pane. He'd thought she might've fallen asleep, and his suspicions were confirmed when he had to gently shake her to wake her up.

"Rory? We're back at the cabins. I need you to sit tight until I open the door and then come help you inside."

She nodded and winced.

Baker met him at the cabin door with a large pizza box in his hands. "I was going to bring tacos, but didn't know how long it would be before you guys got here, so I figured pizza was the safer option."

"It smells great. Thank you." Curtis got the door open, turned on the lights, and grabbed the pillow out of the bedroom Rory had been sleeping in and put it on the couch. "You can set it on the table and make yourself at home. We'll be right in."

He jogged back out to the Jeep and opened the passenger door. "Okay, take it easy." He helped her to ease out of the seat and get to her feet. She wavered a little. Curtis slipped an arm around her waist. "I've got you."

With his foot, he kicked the door and shut it behind them. Inside, he locked the front door, then carefully eased Rory onto the couch near the pillow. She leaned her head back and closed her eyes. "Thank you."

"Of course." He helped her take her shoes off, and she swiveled on the couch so she could lounge against the pillow. "If you need anything, let me know. You're due for more meds in about two hours. Officer Baker brought some pizza. You up for a slice?"

"Definitely. The muffin was good, but I'm starving."

"We'll be back in a few minutes." He resisted the urge to lean in and kiss her.

Instead, he went to the kitchen and found some plates, then pulled several cans of soda from the fridge. "We don't have a lot of choices." He held up a Sprite and a Dr Pepper. "Pick your poison."

Baker pointed to the Sprite. Curtis got another for Rory and a Dr Pepper for himself. Curtis grabbed a chair from the kitchen table and motioned for Baker to take the recliner.

Once they all got food on their plates and were settled, Curtis motioned to the officer. "You've got the floor."

Baker swallowed his bite and gave a nod. "I'm going to just jump right in. We got a set of prints off the fire extinguisher. While they did not pop up in the system, they were a match to those we found outside your trailer window."

"So we know the same person was responsible." Even though they didn't have a name yet, Curtis found the information incredibly satisfying after struggling to put some of the pieces together. "Did any of the security cameras in the mall catch anything?"

"Unfortunately not. When the storm knocked out the power, the generators kicked in to keep the storm shelters lit. The cameras weren't connected to the generator. After you were attacked, Rory, the suspect must have stuck to the maze of hallways because we never saw him on camera leaving the mall." Baker took a drink. "Rory said when she saw him in the storm shelter, he was wearing a blue T-shirt and a baseball cap. Does that sound like the man who attacked her, Curtis?"

Curtis thought back on that moment and finally shook his head, frustrated that he couldn't remember more details.

"I do recall seeing his arms, so he was wearing a short-sleeved shirt. I didn't notice whether he had a cap or not. Honestly, I was focused on the fire extinguisher and Rory."

"The fact is, he could have changed into anything between then and when he left the mall." Baker grabbed another piece of pizza. "Rory, did he say anything to you before you were attacked?"

"No. I never even knew he was there. I was distracted. I'd just gotten off the phone with the little girl's dad and was so relieved that she'd been found. I remember hearing Curtis yell, but then that's it." Rory picked a slice of pepperoni off her pizza and popped it into her mouth. "What I want to know is whether he was watching for me or if he was hiding in the hallways waiting to make a break for it, and I happened to cross his path."

Either way, it was creepy to think about, and Curtis hated that she'd been wandering the hallways on her own in the first place. "We may never know."

"What we do know," Baker began, "is that you saw our suspect at the mall on a Monday afternoon. There's a better chance that he works somewhere in the mall as opposed to being a shopper himself. We're working on compiling a list of mall employees, businesses, and their employees. We're going to get as many pictures as we can. Rory, if you're feeling up to it tomorrow, I'd like you to go through those pictures and see if you recognize anyone. If we have no luck, then you can talk to the sketch artist. See what we get."

"Absolutely. I'll be fine."

Curtis hoped she felt better in the morning. He could tell this meeting was a stretch for her, and he really wanted her to get some rest soon. The doctor had said she shouldn't drive for the next forty-eight hours, which meant if they did go anywhere, Curtis would need to be behind the wheel.

The officer polished off his slice of pizza. "Reach out tomorrow once you've gotten some sleep and rest. Don't feel rushed. Hopefully by then, we'll have even more news for you." He stood. "I'm going to get out of here. We'll have people watching the cabins all night long. Hopefully you can both get some rest."

"Thanks so much." Curtis stood as well and shook Baker's hand. "We appreciate everything you guys are doing."

"I wish we could be doing more faster." Baker gave Rory's shoulder a squeeze.

Curtis walked the officer to the door then made sure it was locked and the security alarm was set. He turned around to find Rory had fallen asleep, her plate still balanced on her stomach, and her head resting on the pillow.

He'd come close to losing her today. Too close.

The killer was getting desperate, and Curtis doubted he was going to stop now.

Chapter Twenty-Two

Curtis didn't have the heart to wake Rory once she fell asleep on the couch last night. She seemed comfortable. Plus, while he knew he didn't technically need to check on her throughout the night since her concussion was a minor one, it made him feel better to be able to quickly see that she was breathing normally. If she'd moved to her room, he would've spent the night worried about her or, if he had gone into her room to make sure she was okay, he definitely would've felt like a creepy stalker.

It was nearing ten in the morning now. They'd both spoken with Karen yesterday afternoon and finally took her up on her offer of time off. They didn't have to go back to work until next Monday. It'd give Rory almost a week to recover.

She was still asleep, and while Curtis was glad she was getting some extra rest, he wanted her to wake up and move around a little. Make sure there weren't any complications from her injuries necessitating a trip to the doctor.

He started making breakfast. Kess had thought of almost everything and had even included a slab of bacon in the supplies she left in the fridge. Curtis had that cooking along with some scrambled eggs. He'd just put some bread in the toaster when he heard shuffling coming from the living room.

Rory had gotten up from the couch and was standing by the table, one hand on it for support.

Curtis turned the eggs and bacon down as low as they could go and rushed to her side. "How are you feeling?"

"Foggy. I'm not dizzy, though, which is a pleasant surprise." She smiled at him.

He smiled back, but his gaze zeroed in on the bruise. It kept getting darker yesterday, but now, there probably wasn't a lot she could do to hide it.

"How bad is it?" Rory gingerly touched the side of her face. "Seriously."

Curtis cupped her chin in his hand and turned her face to the side a little. "You've got a black and purple bruise where the point of impact was, and your eye has decided to match it. A much lighter hue, but yeah."

"I hope the bruising is gone before we go back to work." She sighed. Then her expression brightened when she glanced at the kitchen. "That smells amazing. I'm going to go clean up a little."

"Let me know if you have any dizziness."

"I will. Promise."

When she came back, he was putting food on plates and placing them on the table. He'd also poured each of them a glass of orange juice.

"I had all kinds of pictures in my mind, but seeing my face in the mirror was worse." She wrinkled her nose as she eased into a chair. "I'm going to need to get some makeup before Monday. There's no way this will have faded completely by then."

Curtis joined her and studied her from across the table. She'd brushed her hair, which now fell down her back in a shiny wave. Her pretty eyes looked brighter today, which was a relief. But yeah, looking at her bruise, she was right. She'd be lucky if it had gotten to the yellow shade of healing by then.

He didn't blame her for wanting to cover it up before being out in public much.

"We'll make sure you get what you need before then." He gave her what he hoped was a comforting smile. "For the record, it only makes your face more colorful. Not any less beautiful."

Rory pinned him with a doubtful look, but her cheeks turned pink, and her mouth curved upward. "I'm not sure I believe that, but I'm going to take it." She bit into a strip of bacon and nodded approvingly. "I need to find a way to thank Kess. She's gone above and beyond."

"She really has. I texted her this morning with an update. I also offered to share breakfast with the officer posted in his car outside, but he declined."

Baker had given Curtis a list of the officers who would be watching over the place overnight, along with their phone numbers, in case he needed to contact them directly. It made sense. If they'd had any trouble, the posted officer would be able to respond quicker than if Curtis had to call for help.

They ate their breakfast and seemed to have an unspoken agreement to keep their conversation light-hearted. Rory peppered him with questions about his family, and he enjoyed telling her funny stories about his sisters growing up.

"You're lucky to have so much family," she told him wistfully. "With all of your sisters happily married and raising families, I'm surprised you haven't gone down that road as well." She gave him a curious look, then winced a little. She was probably trying to hide that her head hurt, but Curtis picked up on it.

He stood and retrieved some over-the-counter pain medication and set it on the table in front of her. She gave him a thankful nod and swallowed two pills along with a drink of her orange juice.

"I was engaged once."

Rory's eyes widened, and she leaned into the back of her chair. She reached for the medication bottle and fiddled with it. "What happened?"

"I was young. We were barely twenty, and apparently I was clueless. I thought everything was great between Georgia and me. She called it all off a week before the wedding." Even now, years later, he felt the sting of embarrassment and shock from the memory.

"Ouch. I'm sorry, Curtis. I can't even imagine..." Rory started to shake her head and stopped suddenly, the motion likely causing her head to throb. "It's her loss."

"I appreciate that. She ended up moving to the east coast. Married some other guy two years later." He shrugged. "I'm not going to pretend it didn't hurt, but I know it turned out for the best. If things weren't going to work out between us, I'd rather know that before we got married. Maybe just... a little more than a *week* before."

"I totally get that. A blessing in disguise."

He nodded and finished the rest of his orange juice. "My parents are each other's best friends and have been married for almost forty-five years. They respect each other. They've gone through a lot of challenging things over the years and have always come out stronger on the other side. That's what I want someday. I'd like to think God was looking out for me when it came to the end of my relationship with Georgia. That He had someone else in mind for me."

Until he met Rory, he was starting to wonder whether that last part was true. It was too early in their relationship, and he certainly didn't want to rush things, but she was the first woman that he could see spending his life with. The possibility was both exciting and scary.

"What your parents have is an inspiration. Growing up, I thought marriages like that were just fairy tales." Rory's voice cracked. "Now I would like to think they're much more common than the kind of relationship my parents had."

Curtis reached across the table and took her hand. "The truth is, we can't choose our family or where we start off in life. What we can do is use the positives as a road map leading us on our own path and do everything we can to stop the cycle when it comes to the negative or harmful experiences. They're going to shape us—we can't avoid that —but they don't define us."

Like the way Rory was doing everything she could to better herself, even after the childhood she experienced. She understood that her parents both had problems with addiction, and she wasn't going to allow herself to be put in a position where that might be an issue for her.

He thought about his sister, Lisa. Depression had such a strong hold on her, and no matter what they did, they could never help her break free of it. The fear of someone else he loved going through something similar would be with him forever.

Rory squeezed his hand. "They don't define us. I like that. You know, my mom would tell me all the time never to have kids, because they're a whole lot of work and responsibility. Way more trouble than they're worth."

Her words were soft, as though she had trouble saying them aloud, and the meaning behind them broke Curtis's heart. How many times must she have felt unloved? Unwanted. He sat in his chair and waited for her to continue when what he really wanted to do was circle the table and pull her into his arms. No child should have to doubt their parents' love.

She blinked several times as tears gathered in her eyes. She let go of his hand and ran her thumbs underneath to dry the moisture. "I always thought I'd have my own family. And I'd show my kids every day how important they were and how much I love them. Then maybe my own mom would see things could be different. That they *should* be different."

"Hey." He waited for Rory to look at him. "I've seen how you care for other people and how you face difficult situations. You're an amazing person. That your parents— your mom especially—couldn't see it? That's their loss."

She gave him a wobbly smile and a nod as she wiped away the tears that were racing down her cheeks. "Thank you." She blew out a lungful of air and then slowly got to her feet. The movements didn't seem to cause her as much pain this time.

Curtis looked at his watch. The morning was going by fast. "How are you feeling? Are you up for a trip to the police department?"

"I'm not feeling great, but better after the meds kicked in. Give me a few minutes to wash my face and put my bag together. I can definitely manage the police station, just don't sign me up for a marathon anytime soon."

He chuckled. "I'll try to refrain. I'll give Baker a heads

up that we'll be heading his way." He turned to finish cleaning up, but Rory's voice brought him back around.

"Curtis?"

"Yeah?"

She hesitated. "I've never told anyone about what my mom said to me. Thanks for listening."

"Anytime. I'm always here for you if you need to talk. It was good to get my past with Georgia off my chest, too."

Rory ducked her chin. "I'll be out in a few minutes."

It was an honor to know she trusted him with something she'd never shared with anyone else.

He hoped and prayed that Baker would have some news and that they'd get this case wrapped up before the murderer came after Rory again. Maybe then they could focus on a future where she knew she'd always be safe with him.

Chapter Twenty-Three

As soon as they arrived at the Destiny Police Department, the kind lady out front, Tia, showed them to a conference room and brought them some coffee. "Detective Walker and Officer Baker will be in soon," she assured them before leaving again.

Rory took a sip and savored the flavor. Hopefully the caffeine would kick in and give her a little energy. Maybe it would ease her headache some more in the process.

Medication helped, for sure, but the headache was still there and constant. It was more like pressure that made her want to close her eyes and sleep until it went away. Everything just took more mental effort than it normally would.

Sitting here at the station probably wasn't what Dr. Prescott meant when he said she should take it easy and rest. But once they caught the guys responsible for all of this, she'd have plenty of time to sleep and recover.

Curtis nudged her arm with his. "If you get tired, let me know. We'll leave when you're done. We can always come back later to finish this, or they can come by the cabin."

"Thank you." She rested the uninjured side of her head

against his shoulder and closed her eyes. "I'll be okay. I'm just ready for this nightmare to be over."

"I know, sweetheart. Me, too." He kissed the top of her head and put an arm around her shoulders.

Rory absorbed his warmth and strength. Their conversation back at the cabin had taken a lot out of her. She'd never been that vulnerable with anyone. While she was emotionally spent, she'd also never felt this light before. Knowing that Curtis listened, understood, and didn't judge her was huge.

And then he'd shared something personal with her in return. It was hard to imagine that he'd been engaged before. She'd never met Georgia, but she couldn't fathom a world where she could walk away from Curtis. Certainly not as a friend, much less with the possibility of more developing between them.

The conference room door opened, and Officer Baker came in along with Detective Walker. If either of them were shocked by the bruising on her face, they had the control not to show it. Both men shook their hands and sat down.

"Rory, thank you for coming in after everything that happened yesterday. I was relieved to hear that you're okay." Detective Walker lifted an iPad off a stack of paperwork he'd brought in with him. "We're doubling our efforts to find these guys and get them off the streets before they hurt anyone else."

Baker nodded. "We wanted to update you on the case, then have you go through some photos of people who work at the mall in one capacity or another. Unless he was following you before you got called to the accident in the parking lot, it'd be a huge coincidence that he just happened to be there shopping at the time."

"Agreed." Walker looked up and thanked Tia when she brought him a cup of coffee and Baker a bottle of water. "I finally tracked down the disgruntled customer who was threatening employees at Hoops Artisan Jewelry. He allegedly came in with a gold watch he'd purchased the day before and insisted that it was a fake. He wanted his money back. Employees, on the other hand, said that the watch they sold him was genuine, but the one the customer brought back was clearly a fake. He'd probably sold the watch and then was hoping to get his money back for returning the fake. Double the profit."

Curtis moved his arm from around Rory and reached for his coffee. "He wanted his cake and to eat it, too."

"Exactly. They ended up having to call in mall security to have him escorted from the store." Walker took a drink. "Now here's where it gets interesting. I spoke to the customer and asked him what happened. All he would tell me was that he made a mistake, and that it had been worked out."

"That's weird." Rory wondered if the man had been under some kind of influence at the time.

Baker turned on his own iPad. "We checked into him, and it turns out he's had a lot of financial issues. He's also been arrested for two counts of burglary and one count of drug possession. He's renting a house but is late on the rent more often than not."

"Not exactly the kind of person who's going to go plunk down fifteen grand on a new gold watch." Walker turned his iPad around and showed them a picture of the watch. "Try to sell something like that to make some money, yes, but not buy it."

Rory wasn't exactly well-versed in expensive jewelry, but even she could tell by looking at it that it would be way out of her price range. "So what happened to the watch?"

"We've reached out to all the local pawn shops. Nothing's turned up yet." Baker moved his water and placed it on a blank sheet of paper to keep the condensation from getting the table wet. "It's like the watch never existed in the first place outside of hearsay. There's no record of that kind of money going in or out of his accounts."

"What I'm hoping," Walker looked to Rory and began to pull something else up on his iPad, "is that if you can identify the man who attacked you at the mall, maybe we can connect him to the customer, or it'll lead us in another direction. I've got a lot of photos here for you to look through. Our IT department got photos of everyone they could find who works for the individual stores in the mall as well as for the mall directly. I know it might take some time to go through these, but I think we've got a good shot."

"Of course." She reached for the iPad as the detective handed it over.

One of the things Doctor Prescott had cautioned her about was too much screen time over the next few days because the light would likely intensify her headache. She could feel Curtis's concerned gaze on her as she started to flip through what the album said was almost three hundred images.

Walker had excused himself when a call came in for him, but Baker was sitting quietly on the other side of the table, apparently going through paperwork.

By the time she reached the halfway point, the faces were starting to blend together. Not only that, but her head was beginning to throb to the point that she was feeling a little nauseated.

Curtis leaned closer and lowered his voice. "Hey, maybe you should take a break."

She definitely needed one, but she also needed to get this done. What if the guy who attacked her—who potentially killed the Hoops couple—was in this folder of photos? "Just a few more minutes."

It was clear Curtis disagreed, but instead of voicing his opinion, he gently rubbed the back of her neck. She tried to focus on that instead of the ache in her head and swiped to see the next photograph.

She'd gone through ten or twelve when she swiped again. She gasped as her body tensed.

"That's him."

Chapter Twenty-Four

Curtis lowered his hand from Rory's neck and leaned closer to see the image on the iPad. The man had dark blond hair, was clean shaven, and had almost ice blue eyes. Even in this simple photo, he looked cold. Calculating.

Baker got up from his chair and walked around the conference table to have a look. "You're sure?"

"Without a doubt in my mind." She tapped the screen. "That's the man I saw in the woods, and it's the same guy who was in the storm shelter." She leaned back in her chair and closed her eyes. Looking at the screen for the last forty minutes must have been near torture.

"This is a huge help, Rory. You have no idea. This could be the break in the case we need." Baker took the iPad from her so he could see it closer. "Looks like his name is Nolan Evers. He's the mall manager. Wow, that would make him privy to just about anything happening there. Okay, we'll run his financials and do a full background check on him. See what we can find."

Curtis tapped her knee under the table with his own.

"You did amazing, Rory. Come on. Let's get you back to the cabin."

"Please." She stood and started to lean to one side.

Curtis caught her and guided her back to the chair. "Are you dizzy?"

"Yeah, a little." She looked over at Officer Baker. "I'm sorry. It was the screen. My head is killing me. Concussions —I don't recommend them." She tried to chuckle, but it sounded more like a groan.

"Please don't apologize. I'm just sorry we had to ask you to look at them in the first place. If you'd like, we have a family room with a couch where you can rest for a bit. You can close the door, and the lights are on a dimmer, so you can adjust that as well. Maybe some rest in dim lighting will help."

If she was struggling with the lights in here, Curtis didn't want to think about how painful the sunshine outside might be. He was relieved when she agreed.

"The family room sounds great."

"Let me show you where it is." Baker gathered everything on the table.

Curtis helped Rory stand and then put an arm around her waist. He hated that she felt bad enough to rest her head against his shoulder, but he was glad she felt comfortable enough to do so. If he didn't think it'd embarrass her, he'd be tempted to scoop her up and just carry her.

Baker led them down the hall. "Now, don't let the fact that it's the same general area as the medical examiner deter you. The family room is for those who might have to come in and identify a body, so they have some privacy. But it's also used regularly for people who have to stay late or just need a quiet place to do some research."

It all made sense, though it was still odd to be walking

into the same area as the morgue. The room, however, was very homey. Curtis helped her ease down to the couch. The moment she sank onto the cushions, he could see the tension flow right out of her body. She reached for one of the decorative pillows and clutched it to her chest.

"Stay as long as you need. When you're ready, just let me know, and I'll walk you back out." With that, Baker closed the door behind them, leaving them alone in silence.

Rory closed her eyes, shutting out the light, and took a deep breath.

"You could lie down," Curtis suggested. "I can sit in the chair over there. Or even leave and wait outside if it helps you rest better."

"Will you sit with me? After you dim the lights? I'm not going to be able to stay awake, but I don't want to be here alone. I just need a few minutes to rest my eyes..."

Curtis didn't want to leave her either. Instead, he dimmed the lights until he could barely make out the furniture in the room.

As soon as he sat on the couch beside her, she curled her body against him, the palm of her hand pressed against his chest. Her breathing evened out in seconds. Curtis considered easing her into a more comfortable position where she could rest her head on one of the decorative pillows, but he was more concerned about waking her up than anything. Surely, if she got uncomfortable, she'd try to change positions on her own.

Instead, he held her and prayed silently for God to heal her brain and ease the pain and nausea. For the police to catch Nolan Evers and the man he was working with. Finally, he prayed that, if there was going to be something more than friendship between him and Rory, God would work it out.

Because right now, he couldn't fathom not having her in his life.

"You obviously needed the rest."

Poor Rory had been shocked when she realized she'd not only fallen asleep in the family room at the morgue, but that she'd slept solidly for more than two hours.

"Yes, but you had to just sit there. You could've woken me up after a reasonable amount of time." She looked at him as though he'd somehow lost his mind.

Curtis chuckled. "Are you upset that I let you sleep, or embarrassed that you fell asleep on me?"

Her face turned pink, giving him his answer.

He stepped forward and gently cupped her upper arms. "Rory, after as bad as you felt, two hours seemed like a reasonable amount of time to me. Do you feel better?"

She stopped and seemed to take stock of her symptoms. "Yes. My head doesn't hurt nearly as bad as it did before."

"Well, there you go then. Besides, I'd be lying if I said I didn't doze off for a while myself."

Rory folded her arms. "That does make me feel a little better."

"I'll message Baker. We can go upstairs, get you a bottle of water so you can take some meds, and see if they've found anything else about Evers."

"Yeah, that sounds good."

Less than ten minutes later, they were back in the conference room. Rory took her medication, and Officer Baker brought in a box of scones that he put on the table and pushed their direction. "Please help yourselves.

Someone was kind enough to bring several boxes in not long ago."

Curtis wasn't hungry, but Rory reached for one that looked like cinnamon swirl.

"I know you're ready to get back to the cabin and rest, but I wanted to share what we've found out about Evers. He's been working at the mall for the last fifteen years. He held the position of Assistant Mall Manager until about five years ago, when he stepped up as Manager. He's got a wife and a son who's eight."

The conference room door opened, and Detective Walker joined them. "Where are we at?"

"I was just telling them about Evers' position at the mall and his family."

Walker chose a scone but didn't take a bite as he walked to the other side of the table. "We're trying to locate him and his family, but they aren't at home, and their cell phones have been turned off. According to the school where his son usually attends, he didn't show up for class yesterday or today. His mother had called and told them he was sick."

"You think they're running." Rory picked at her scone. "Do they have any other family in the area?"

Evers probably thought he had no choice but to run. Up until he'd used the fire extinguisher to hit Rory, he might have been able to claim that he had a part in the crimes but hadn't actually pulled the trigger. It was too late for that now. If nothing else, attempted murder was one of the many charges the police would bring against him.

"None nearby." Baker frowned. "We have reached out to the extended family that we know of and let them know that we need to speak to Evers. But they're more likely to protect him and his family than they are to turn him in. We've also got a BOLO out on their missing vehicle."

"We're waiting on a warrant to come through. Once we have that, we'll go through his house and office at the mall," Walker assured them. "Meanwhile, we've been looking into his financials. There's a large savings account in his son's name, another in his wife's, plus an offshore account. A lot of money goes in and out of that offshore account, but it's been routed through so many banks that we're having a difficult time getting specific information."

Curtis would have felt a lot better if they knew where the guy was. "I'm not surprised he took off. I *am* a little surprised that it looks like he may have taken his family with him. It'd be a lot easier to disappear if he were alone."

"You're not wrong. I'm hoping he'll be easier to find if they're together." Walker tore off a chunk of his scone. "In the meantime, we'll keep digging. There has to be a connection between Evers and the other man who was in the woods. We're going to find it." He popped the bite into his mouth.

"We truly appreciate your help," Baker said. "I'll be in touch, and please reach out if either of you needs anything." He shook Curtis's hand and gave Rory's arm a pat. "Come on. I'll show you guys out. We'll have a patrol car come back out this evening to keep watch tonight."

By the time they were back in the Jeep and driving away from the Police Department, it felt like they'd been there for days. He looked over at Rory to see how she was doing. Hopefully the fact she wasn't squinting was a good sign. "You feeling okay? Do you need anything before we get back to the cabin?"

"I'm making it." She met his gaze and smiled. "Thank

you for worrying about me. I've never really had that before."

It was still hard for him to grasp that fact. She deserved to be looked after. He knew there was a lot they still didn't know about each other, and it would take time to get to best friend status, but he hoped he could be the one to step into that role.

Which meant he needed to talk to her about his plans to join the fire department. Thinking about that conversation made him nervous, though it was hard for him to put into words exactly why.

"You're unusually quiet over there." Rory was watching him curiously.

"Do you want some ice cream? I thought we could stop at a drive-through before heading back. With the temperatures getting warmer now that it's almost the end of April, it makes me think of ice cream season."

"Is ice cream ever out of season?"

"Touché."

"Come on, Curtis. What is it? If you need to get back to work, I totally get that. You don't need to babysit me." The curiosity on her face had morphed into concern.

He hadn't even broached the subject yet, and already it wasn't going well. They approached one of Destiny's many public parks and pulled in, finding a spot beneath one of the large shade trees. Hopefully that would lessen the sunlight enough to keep Rory's headache at bay.

Curtis turned in his seat to face her. "There's something I need to talk to you about."

Chapter Twenty-Five

Rory's mind raced through the possible topics that Curtis might want to talk about. He looked nervous—or at least as nervous as she'd ever seen him look. Considering he always seemed to easily command the situations he was faced with, this was definitely unusual.

She was joking about him not feeling as though he had to babysit her. What if that's exactly how he felt?

"Okay. What's up? Do I need to be worried?"

"No. I'm sorry. This was supposed to be a casual conversation over ice cream back at the cabin." He reached for her hand, weaving his fingers with hers. "I always knew I wanted to be an EMT, even when I was a kid. It was a no-brainer for me, and I've always enjoyed the work. A couple of years ago, I started feeling the need to improve. To learn more. That's what led me to go through the program and become a paramedic."

He was a talented one, too. She'd seen it more times than she could count. Curtis saved lives and made a difference every single day.

169

Watching him do the work to become a paramedic had inspired her to consider going down that same road in the future. She gave him an encouraging nod to continue.

"Lately, I've been feeling like I'm doing the right thing, but I'm not in the right place." He paused as though he were trying to choose the right words. "I want to become a paramedic for the fire department. It's going to be a lot. I'll need to get my firefighter certification and then actually go through the hiring process."

He looked down at their joined hands. "I have no idea how long all of that will take, or if I'll be able to continue my job at the hospital while I'm working on it. I just know that the decision feels right." He pressed her hand before looking up at her. "I'm going to desperately miss working with you. The last thing I want is for you to feel like I'm abandoning you. I guess I want to know what you think."

Working with Curtis was one of her favorite parts of the day. She'd really miss him. But she could totally see him being a fire department paramedic, and it suited him.

"I think you should do whatever you feel called to do. The Destiny Fire Department would be lucky to have you. I have no doubt that you'll ace any certification or tests they put in front of you."

Curtis started to say something, then stopped. "The thing is, we haven't talked about any of this." He lifted their joined hands in case she had any doubt about what *this* meant. "I want to see where this is going. I don't want my leaving the hospital—and us no longer working together—to sabotage anything."

Her heart pounded as the true weight of his words settled over her like the whisper of a promise that she desperately wanted to cling to.

"You wouldn't be abandoning me. Where you work

wouldn't change anything between us. Not really. And for the record? I really want to see where this thing of ours is going, too."

He used his other hand to gently lift her chin before leaning in and kissing her. It was the kind of kiss that started off soft, sweet, and full of new promises. Then he deepened it, making Rory wish there wasn't a console between them so she could feel his strong arms around her to keep her from floating away.

When he broke their kiss, he rested his forehead against hers. "Thank you for being supportive. I always want us to be friends before anything else. Because if we have that…"

"I know. That's important to me, too." She leaned forward for one more kiss. It was brief, but still had her heart beating a mile a minute. She leaned back against her seat. "You know, this is all probably going to be easier if we work at different places anyway. I'm not sure Karen would support us driving around in the same rig otherwise."

"I'd thought about that, too. Not to mention I could legally carry my firearm if I chose to. I have to say, it would've come in handy more than once over the last few days." Curtis lifted their joined hands and placed a kiss against the back of hers. "So ice cream, then back to the cabin?"

"That sounds like a plan."

They went through the drive-through so Rory didn't have to deal with people staring at the bruises on her face. They'd probably have taken one look at her and thought Curtis was the one who hurt her. He had to admit he might've come to that conclusion first himself if roles were reversed.

Instead of trying to get back to the cabin before their ice cream melted, or trying to eat his while he drove, they opted to sit in the parking lot and enjoy their cones.

As soon as their treats were gone, Curtis put the Jeep in drive. He was thankful the nap at the police department helped with Rory's headache, but he knew it would likely be back before long. He'd rather get her to the cabin before that happened.

They talked about random things along the way until he pulled up in front of Rory's cabin. He went around the Jeep to help her out. She winced when her feet touched the ground, and he was glad they hadn't stayed in town any longer than they did.

With an arm loosely around her waist, he helped her to the cabin door. She unlocked it, and he put in the passcode to disarm the security system.

Curtis was just closing the door again when a shoe shoved its way between the door and the jamb, causing the door to bounce right off of it with a thud.

Before he could reach for the handgun in the holster at his back, Nolan Evers pushed his way inside, his own gun in his hands.

"Don't even think about it, or you'll be the first person I shoot. Put your gun on the floor and slide it to me. Slowly."

Curtis hated the idea of being unarmed. Right now, there was no way for him to draw his weapon and take Nolan out without jeopardizing Rory's life. He clenched his jaw and did exactly as the other man asked.

Nolan carefully picked up the gun and stuck it into the waistband of his pants. "Good. Now take your phones and your smartwatches and put them on that little table there. Then sit down. Both of you." He motioned toward the dining room table with his gun.

"It's going to be okay," Curtis told Rory under his breath. He chose the seat facing Nolan. Rory was calm as she sat down, but the fear in her eyes was unmistakable.

"Don't move." Nolan jabbed the gun at them, then turned back to the front door. He stuck his other hand out, and a moment later, a woman carrying a young boy came inside. Nolan closed and locked the front door behind them.

Curtis exchanged a confused look with Rory. Why would Nolan bring his family here? The guy was dangerous enough as it was, but to have his wife and son with him now? Having someone you love in a tense situation like this was going to bring out a forceful need to defend them and keep them safe.

Curtis knew that firsthand. He wished he could somehow reassure Rory that everything was going to be all right. It had to be, because he refused to lose what he had with her before it'd even had the chance to begin.

The boy looked to be about seven, and he had his arms wrapped around his mom's neck. His eyes were wide as he looked from his dad to Curtis and Rory.

Nolan's expression softened noticeably when he looked at them. "My son's not feeling well. Is there a bed in the back where he can rest?"

That was the last thing Curtis expected him to say. Why not keep his family there in the living room where he could keep an eye on them? "Sure. Either bedroom is fine."

Nolan nodded to his wife, who carried their son out of the room. "I'm banking on the fact that at least one of you has your medical gear here. I need you to figure out what's wrong with my boy." His gaze hardened as he focused on Rory.

Curtis immediately shook his head. "We're not doing anything for you while you've got that gun pointed at us."

"And I'm thinking you're not in the position to say no. Not if you both want to walk out of this alive. Do you have medical supplies here, or not?"

Normally, Curtis's kit would be out in his Jeep, but he'd been bringing it inside just in case he needed anything for Rory. He'd much rather be overprepared than not have something he needed. He looked to Rory again, who gave a subtle nod.

"Yes, my medical gear is over there on the other side of the couch."

Nolan kept his gun trained on them while he backed up and checked to see that the large duffel full of supplies was there. He aimed his gun right at Rory. "I want you to take this and go check on my son."

Anger flared in Curtis's chest. "Leave her alone. I'll do it."

"You're going to sit right here. Your cooperation is what will guarantee her safety."

"No. She's in no condition. Look at her face." It took everything in Curtis not to rise from his chair. "You gave her a concussion when you decided to hit her over the head with that fire extinguisher. She needs to rest."

There was slight hesitation in Nolan's eyes before his steel expression slid right back into place. "This isn't a negotiation. You help my son feel well enough to travel, we'll leave, and you'll both walk out of here. Refuse, and there's no reason for me to leave either of you alive."

Chapter Twenty-Six

Nolan Evers was desperate. He had to be to come by the cabin and take them hostage instead of trying to get as far away from Destiny as he could. Surely, he could have taken his son to an urgent care center somewhere for treatment. Why risk everything by coming here?

All Rory knew was that they had few options. They were facing an armed man who was demanding something for his family. He wasn't going to back down.

"It's okay. I'll check on your son. But if I do that, I need you to stay calm. Like you said, we all just want to walk away from this."

She avoided looking at Curtis for fear of changing her mind. She wanted Nolan to see that she was determined and more than capable of doing as he asked. Besides, if his wife started talking, then maybe Rory could find out where they planned to go. Even if they had to let them leave, having a possible destination meant the police could catch up with them there.

Nolan looked at his watch and shifted his weight from

one foot to the other. "Get a move on. We don't have much time."

Curtis must've noticed Nolan's nervousness, too. "Why? How much time do we have to work with?"

Their captor's brows rose as he waved his gun at Rory and growled out, "Get moving. Help my son. If you try to leave this house, or if you hurt my wife or son, I'll kill your boyfriend here. Do you understand what I'm saying?"

Rory nodded quickly. "Yes. I understand." She stood slowly, and her stomach rolled with nausea. Whether it was because of her head injury or the nerves, she had no way of knowing. She held her hands up where he could see them and walked to retrieve Curtis's medical supplies.

Nolan raised his voice. "Shelly, the woman doctor is coming your way. If she gives you any trouble at all, you let me know."

"I've got it." The wife's voice was even. Determined.

Rory's gaze tangled with Curtis's. He mouthed, "Be careful."

She gave a subtle nod. Turning her back on Nolan and walking away from Curtis was one of the hardest— and scariest—things Rory had ever done. Knowing that Curtis was facing the barrel of that gun and that everything hinged on whether she could figure out what was wrong with the boy brought another wave of nausea. She sent up a silent prayer that God would keep them both safe.

Shelly was standing in the doorway to Rory's bedroom. Rory kept her hands up. For all she knew, the wife was armed, too.

Inside the room, the little boy was lying on his side on the bed facing the door, his legs pulled up, and a look of misery on his face. His mother had dumped out the small wastebasket beside the bed, and it sat next to him on the bed.

"I'm going to set the bag down and get some supplies out. What's been going on with your son?"

"Just fix him. Please." Shelly wrung her hands together and walked to the foot of the bed then back to where her son was.

Rory found the stethoscope, blood pressure cuff, oximeter, otoscope, and thermometer. She placed them all on the edge of the bed.

"I want to help him, but to do that as quickly as possible, I need to know what's been going on. How long has he been sick? What are his symptoms?" Rory glanced at the iPad sitting on the side table. She'd left it there the last time she used it. There was no way she could contact anyone with it, but maybe Curtis could. If she had the opportunity to grab it and get it to him, she'd take it.

The little boy never took his eyes off Rory.

Shelly walked around the bed to the other side and back again. "He says his stomach hurts all the time. He's thrown up several times. He's had a fever, and he doesn't want to eat anything. I thought it might be the stomach flu. It's been going around his school a lot this spring. But now, he cries when he tries to stand up." She gathered her long, dark hair in both hands and brought it over her shoulder where she fiddled with it absently. Her brown eyes glittered with unshed tears.

"When did these symptoms start?" It did sound like it could be the flu, but it could be a host of other things, too.

"Last night."

"I'm going to examine your son. I think it'd make him feel more at ease if I knew his name. Can you tell me what that is?"

Shelly hesitated. "Braden."

"Good, thank you, Shelly. If you'd like to sit with Braden, that might make him feel more comfortable, too."

She sat on the other side of the bed and rubbed her son's back.

Rory knelt on the floor beside the bed and tried to ignore the way her head throbbed. "Hi, Braden. My name is Rory. I'm going to give you a little check-up and see if we can figure out why you're hurting. Does that sound okay?"

The little boy looked over his shoulder at his mother. When she patted him on the shoulder, he nodded at Rory.

Rory made sure to tell them what she was doing first before taking Braden's vitals. The more she put the pair at ease, the better.

"Is everything going okay in there, Shelly?"

Nolan's raised voice startled Rory, and she nearly dropped the oximeter.

"Yes. She's giving Braden a check-up to see what's going on." Shelly's gaze went from the door to Rory. "His back's up against a wall. He's just trying to protect our family. Nolan is a good man. A good father."

"I'm sure he is."

Rory must not have sounded convincing enough, because her comment earned her a sharp look.

"Okay, sweetie, I'm going to put this on your finger. This will tell me how much oxygen is in your blood. That's pretty cool, isn't it?"

Braden looked at the way the device's glow made the tip of his finger red and nodded. "You don't have to take out my blood?"

It was the first time the boy had spoken, and Rory considered that great progress. She smiled at him. "Nope. You get to keep all of your blood."

He grimaced and drew his knees closer to his body.

Rory waited for the oximeter to finish its reading then addressed Shelly. "Braden's oxygen levels are great. His ears are clear, and his heart and lungs sound good. He does have a fever of 102. That's pretty high, but it could be worse. It does tell me that his body is fighting something, whether it's a virus like the stomach flu or some kind of infection, I can't really know without running some tests that I don't have access to here."

"Then how do we find out?" Shelly smoothed some of her son's dark hair away from his forehead. His hair and eyes were the same color as his mom's, but his physical characteristics were similar to his dad's. He was a perfect combination of the two.

"I need to feel his belly. I'll be able to tell where he's actually hurting. I can learn a lot from the way his stomach feels, too." She focused on Braden. "I promise I'll be careful. If something hurts, you just have to tell me."

Braden didn't look convinced. "What happened to your face?"

Rory had forgotten how badly she was bruised. The poor kid. That probably scared him as much as anything else that'd happened this evening.

She caught a worried look from Shelly. Did she know that her husband had caused Rory's injuries?

As far as Rory could tell, Braden was well taken care of, and he trusted his parents. Making him fear his dad now would only make things worse. "I hit my head on something really hard. But it's just a bruise. It'll go away. It might take a little while."

Braden held out his tiny arm to show off a green and yellow bruise near his elbow. "Like mine."

"Yes, just like yours. Mine will turn green and yellow,

too. Then it'll go away. I'll bet yours doesn't even hurt anymore, does it?"

The boy shook his head.

"All right, is it okay if I check your tummy now?"

He nodded and shifted to lie on his back, but it was clear the position was causing him pain.

"If anything hurts, you just tell me, and I'll stop."

The little boy nodded again. Rory didn't have to touch his abdomen to tell that he was bloated. "Has Braden been able to go to the bathroom normally?"

"No. I figured it was because he wasn't eating."

"That could definitely be part of it." Rory focused on the boy's response to her examination. He seemed to have pain around his belly button down to the lower right side and into his lower back.

She was no doctor, and there were several things this could be, but she was confident the boy had appendicitis. It was impossible to tell how bad it was. One thing was certain, though. Braden needed more help than she was able to give. He needed a hospital and a surgeon before his symptoms worsened and his appendix ruptured.

Fear coiled in her chest. What would Nolan do when he found out she wasn't going to be able to fix his son?

Chapter Twenty-Seven

Curtis hated not knowing how Rory was doing. Judging from the way Nolan kept looking down the hall toward the bedrooms, he wasn't a fan of being in the dark, either. Rory had always been good with her patients, but that was especially true when it came to children. If anyone had a chance of befriending Nolan's wife and son, it was her.

"Can you see them?"

"What?" Nolan's eyes narrowed.

"Can you see them? Does Rory look like she's doing okay?"

Irritation flared in his eyes. "I'm not concerned about her."

"Maybe you should be. If she passes out from pain, then you're going to have to let me go in and treat them both. I can promise you, Rory will be my priority."

Nolan looked like he was going to say something else, then chose to remain silent. He shifted over several feet and looked down the hallway again. "She looks fine." He pressed his lips into a thin line. "I didn't hit her. That wasn't me."

Curtis blinked at him as he processed what he'd said. "Rory saw you in the storm shelter."

"Yes, I was there. But I'm not the one who hit her." The muscles in his jaw flexed as though he were forcefully closing his mouth to keep from saying too much.

"You're saying the person you're working with is the one who hit my partner in the head with a fire extinguisher?" Curtis wanted to doubt him. The truth was, they had no idea who the other suspect was, and Curtis never did see the man's face after he'd tried to kill Rory.

Nolan stood, feet firmly planted, his gun at the ready.

If Curtis could keep the man talking, then maybe he could learn about the partner. "We know you're not the one who shot the Hoops." For the first time, Curtis noticed that the man was carrying a 9 mm pistol. "The gun you have now isn't even the same kind of gun that was used to kill them. Who did it, then? Because he seems to be content to let you take the fall. The police have been able to tie you to a number of crimes, and I'm willing to bet that the fingerprints found on Rory's trailer before you burned it down belong to you."

Nolan only pierced Curtis with a stare that revealed very little about what he was thinking. He glanced at his watch again, and his grip on the gun tightened. An armed man who was desperate, with a time constraint. Not good.

Even if Curtis had the opportunity to rush him and take the gun, that would leave Rory defenseless in the other room. He had no doubt she could handle Shelly Evers in a normal situation, but Rory was injured. Plus, Shelly would protect her son at all costs. There was no telling what she'd do.

No, he needed to be in the same room as Rory before he tried to gain control. Until then, he needed to either de-escalate the situation or find a way to contact Baker.

"The way I see it, if you didn't murder the Hoops couple, and you're not the one who actually physically attacked Rory, then there's someone else. Someone who seems to be calling all the shots, and whom you seem to want to get your family away from. If he wants Rory dead—a woman who had nothing to do with any of this—then do you really think he's just going to let you leave town and not try to come after you, too?"

"Quiet." The word was a low growl.

"You clearly love your family and want to protect them. That woman in there—the one who's injured and trying to help your son? I love her, too. Protecting her and making sure she stays safe is all I want."

Nolan looked in the direction of the bedrooms again. "As soon as my son can travel and I know he'll be okay, we'll leave. I don't want to hurt anyone."

Anger flared in Curtis. "Slashing Rory's tires, burning her home down, and leaving a threatening note. I wouldn't call that not hurting someone. That's assuming I believe you weren't the one who physically tried to kill her."

"She was living in a travel trailer. I was hoping she'd be scared enough to leave town. Go stay with family or something. Then he—" Nolan's jaw snapped shut.

Curtis's mind ran through different scenarios. Nolan clearly felt trapped now. What if that'd always been the case? Obviously, it still didn't excuse his actions. If he'd gone to the police, they could've offered protection for his family. But sometimes the situation isn't nearly as black and white when you're in the middle and trying to fight your way out of it.

"Who's threatening your family? Who wants to kill Rory?"

Nolan's eyes narrowed. "Shelly? Is she helping Braden?"

"Mr. Evers?" Rory's voice rose from the other room. "I think I know what's going on with Braden. I'd like to come out there and speak to you and Shelly. Is that okay?"

"I need you to fix my boy."

"And I need to be able to tell you the options without him overhearing the conversation."

Worry immediately flashed across Nolan's face.

Curtis wondered whether there was something seriously wrong with the boy or if Rory was just trying to find a way to get back into the living room again.

"Come back in here then. Slow movements."

A moment later, Rory reappeared. She held her hands up in front of her. She approached the table and sat stiffly in the chair she'd used before.

Shelly walked into the room and stood next to her husband. She stared at the gun in his hand for several moments before focusing on Rory. "What's wrong with Braden?"

Rory's hands shook a little. Curtis reached over and clasped one of them in his.

"Braden has a high fever, he hasn't been eating well, and he has a great deal of pain in his abdomen. I'm afraid he has acute appendicitis, given the symptoms and how long he's not felt well. He needs to go to the hospital."

Nolan immediately shook his head. "No. There has to be something else you can do. Can you give him some antibiotics so he's well long enough for us to get out of town?"

Shelly hugged herself and looked toward the bedroom.

"There's truly nothing we can do for him here." Rory gripped Curtis's hand. "He might be okay for another day or two. Or his appendix could burst five minutes from now. Once it bursts, it'll lead to a serious infection. If not treated immediately, he could develop abscesses, sepsis, and organ damage." She turned her attention from Nolan to Shelly. "This could kill him."

Shelly clutched Nolan's free arm. "Nolan, please. We can't risk it."

"I know. But if we go to one of the hospitals in Destiny, he's going to find us. He may find us here if we don't get moving soon."

Their situation was bad enough. What Curtis didn't want to happen was to have the other person involved—the one who had actually murdered people—come charging into the cabin. He'd already proven he didn't hesitate to kill. If Nolan told the truth, and it was his partner who attacked Rory in the mall, then the only reason he'd hit her with the fire extinguisher instead of just shooting her was because he was afraid someone would hear the shot.

Rory nudged his knee with hers. She let go of his hand and reached behind her body to slowly lift the back of her shirt. She pulled something out and moved it under the table, placing it on his lap.

Curtis felt the object with his hand. His iPad. She must have snuck it from her bedroom. He'd be sure to kiss her and tell her how much he appreciated her plan as soon as all of this was over.

If he could turn the iPad on and go to his login, then he could contact Baker. All his texts were linked from his phone to his iPad, and he could use either to send or receive.

The couple was talking in harsh whispers. Shelly was in tears now, and Nolan was clearly conflicted.

While they were distracted, Curtis turned the iPad on and immediately turned down the volume and dimmed the screen as low as it would go. Then he logged in on his own account. That was as far as he could go because Nolan turned his attention to them again.

Curtis left the iPad balanced on his lap and made sure both of his hands were above the table.

"Mommy?" Braden's little voice called from the other room. "My tummy hurts." The unmistakable sound of a child vomiting followed.

Shelly gave her husband a pointed look and hurried to her son.

Rory rubbed the back of her neck with one hand and winced. "Look, Nolan. The way I see it, you have two choices. You can take Braden to the hospital here and get him help right away, or you can try to make it to the hospital in a different town."

Curtis took a moment to study her face. She was tired and hurting. She was also one of the bravest people he'd ever met. He turned his focus on Nolan. "If you're worried your partner is going to find you and harm your family, then we can contact the police. They'll make sure your family is kept safe. Take your partner in custody."

"And I'll go to jail, too. I won't be there for my family. For my son." His words were bitter, but there was a resigned look on his face.

"If what you said was true, and you didn't commit murder or try to kill Rory, then your sentence will be minimal. It sounds like you were coerced to a point, and the judge will take that into consideration. It's better that your son visits you in jail until you're released to rejoin your family than for you to lose your son. Especially when, right now, you have the ability to save his life." Curtis prayed his words would hit their mark and not anger the man who still held a gun and was clearly backed into a corner. A dangerous combination.

Nolan looked toward the bedroom. "Shelly, how is he?"

Curtis quickly scooted his chair a few inches away from the table and looked down at the iPad on his lap. He opened his texts and touched Baker's name. As quickly as he could, he typed out, "9-1-1. Cabin. Evers gun." As soon as he sent the text, he brought his hands back into view. He reached for Rory's hand and gave her a subtle nod. He prayed that Baker would see the text and that help was on the way.

As soon as Shelly came back into the living room, the sound of an engine came from in front of the cabin. A car door opened and slammed shut. Nolan immediately swung his gun from the kitchen table to the front door.

There's no way it could be the police. Not that quickly.

Someone pounded on the front door. "Evers! Show your face, or I'll burn this cabin down and your family with it!"

Chapter Twenty-Eight

Curtis gave Rory's hand a tight squeeze and whispered, "I'm going to make sure you and Shelly are in the back room with Braden. Barricade the door and stay low."

"I'm not going to leave you in here." Fear laced her voice as she gripped his hand, her eyes pleading with him to change his mind.

"I need you to trust me, and Shelly and Braden need you to keep them safe."

She finally nodded her agreement.

Nolan kept his eyes on the door, but he used his free hand to guide Shelly toward the bedroom. "Go in with Braden."

"Nolan!" Curtis spoke loud enough to get the man's attention. "I need Rory to go back there, too."

The other man looked his way briefly, his gaze flicking to Rory. He nodded. "Go."

Rory stood and, with one last look at Curtis, hurried with Shelly into the bedroom. He heard the door close and prayed they stayed safe until all of this was over.

More pounding on the front of the cabin. "Evers! Did you hear me?"

Curtis rose from the table, earning him a frantic look from Nolan and the focus of his gun. "Listen to me, Nolan. The police are on the way." He set the iPad on top of the kitchen table. "Who's out there? At this point, we just need to stay alive long enough for help to get here."

There was a brief moment where Nolan seemed to go through his options, but he must've realized the truth of Curtis's words.

"It's Victor Hoops. He killed his own brother and sister-in-law. He won't hesitate to kill the rest of us." He swung his gun back to face the front door.

"I need my gun." When the other man shook his head, Curtis stepped around the table. "Listen to me, I give you my word that my primary focus will be holding Victor off until the police get him into custody."

More pounding on the door.

Nolan finally nodded, withdrew Curtis's gun, and held it out.

Curtis took it from him. "Thank you." He moved toward the table where their phones were still waiting. "I need to let the police know what they're walking into." He didn't wait for permission to snatch his phone, dial Baker's number, and put it on speaker.

"Baker here. I'm on the way with additional units. Are you guys okay?"

"No. The situation has escalated. Rory and I are in the cabin along with Nolan Evers, his wife, and their son. Nolan's partner, Victor Hoops, is outside threatening to kill everyone. According to Nolan, Victor is the one who shot his brother and tried to kill Rory."

"Understood. Is Victor alone?"

"We don't know." Curtis held the phone closer and spoke in a lower tone. "Rory and Nolan's family are in one of the bedrooms. We're going to need an ambulance for the little boy. He's suffering from acute appendicitis."

He looked over at Nolan, who gave a nod.

"Got it. We're less than five minutes out."

Curtis tossed the phone onto the nearest surface and focused on the door. "Victor, the police are on their way. This isn't going to end the way you want it to."

A deep, humorless laugh cut its way through the door. "No, it's certainly not."

"He has billions of dollars at stake," Nolan ground out. "His family's been running a money laundering business out of the jewelry store for years. That's all over now, but all Victor can think about is revenge. I'm convinced he'd sell his wife and kids if that's what it took to keep the business going." He made no effort to lower his voice. He was as much talking to Victor as he was telling Curtis anything.

Victor fired two shots at the door. One went wide, but the other came way too close to hitting Nolan. The bullet slammed into the wall behind them.

Curtis prayed that, if Rory and the others weren't out of the house, that they would stay low to the ground.

He dropped low, and Nolan did the same, but they kept their weapons trained on the door.

"Greg was weak!" Victor yelled as he shot another round through the door. "Dad handed us a fortune on a silver platter, but Greg wanted out. He was going to ruin everything."

Victor tried the doorknob again with a roar.

Curtis got Nolan's attention. If Victor came through the door, they were going to have to end the confrontation immediately because it was clear Victor would have no qualms killing them all. He said nothing, but Nolan must have been thinking along the same lines because he clenched his jaw and returned his attention to the door.

Three more shots obliterated the doorknob, followed immediately by the sound of the door splintering as Victor kicked it in.

Curtis was prepared to shoot the moment Victor entered the cabin, but Officer Baker's voice boomed from outside. "Victor Hoops, this is the police. Drop the gun and raise your hands. Do it now."

Victor leveled a piercing gaze on Curtis, then swung it to Nolan. Rage contorted his face into something inhuman as he leveled his gun at Nolan.

Before he had a chance to pull the trigger, several shots came from behind Victor. His eyes widened as he fell forward and hit the floor, his gun skidding across the wooden planks.

Baker approached the door cautiously, his weapon drawn and aimed at Nolan. "I need you to place your gun on the floor and put your hands behind your head."

Curtis held his breath and prayed that Nolan would make the right choice. There was no other way out of this scenario.

Nolan only hesitated a moment before he lowered the gun. "Yeah. I'm putting it down. Don't shoot." As soon as the gun was at his feet, he stood again and linked his fingers behind his head. "Please, I need to check on my family."

Baker entered the cabin immediately followed by Detective Walker and Officer Carrington. Baker took custody of Nolan, placing his hands behind him and securing cuffs. Carrington knelt to check Victor's pulse and shook his head.

Curtis set his own handgun down on the small table so

he was unarmed as well. He motioned to Nolan. "He never fired a shot. Not at me or at Victor."

He still wasn't sure whether Nolan was a bad man who had finally made the right decision, or if he was a good man that had allowed himself to be caught up in a rough situation. Curtis caught the officer's attention. "Baker, I'm going to check on the others."

"Yep." He spoke into his radio. "Situation is clear. Have the ambulance come on through."

Curtis ran to the closed bedroom door. "Rory, it's Curtis. Baker's here, and everything is under control."

Shuffling sounds followed by scrapes told him they were moving a piece of furniture out from in front of the door. The lock clicked. The moment Rory stepped out, Curtis pulled her into his arms.

"Thank you, God," he breathed as he relished the fact she was safe and sound.

"Are you okay?" Her words were muffled against his shirt. She leaned back. "We heard the shots..."

"I'm fine." He looked in the room where Shelly was holding her son on the floor. Her eyes were wide and filled with tears. "Nolan is okay, too."

Shelly burst into tears and cradled her son in her arms.

"Victor?" Rory asked the question, but it was clear she already knew the answer.

Curtis simply shook his head as a siren pierced the air. "That's an ambulance for Braden."

Rory hugged him close again and pressed a quick kiss to his lips before moving further into the room. She knelt beside mother and son. "Braden, they're going to take you and your mom to the hospital where some really nice doctors are going to help you feel better."

Curtis stepped aside so the EMTs could come in with

the stretcher. Once they had the boy ready for transport, he moved into the living area where he and several officers created a visual barrier so Braden didn't have to see Victor's body. The poor kid had already been through enough.

Rory and Curtis followed them out of the house, and she waved as they loaded the little boy into the ambulance. Baker allowed Nolan the chance to say goodbye to his son and his wife before she got in after Braden, and the ambulance was on its way.

It was going to be a long evening with statements to give and a mess to clean up. Curtis folded Rory into his arms, breathed in the smell of shampoo, and welcomed the warmth of her embrace. At least this nightmare was over.

Chapter Twenty-Nine

Rory accepted a tall glass of sweet, iced tea from Kess then took a sip. It had the perfect amount of sugar in it and was exactly what she needed to quench her thirst. "This is great. Thank you."

"Are you kidding? It's the least I can do since you and my brother insist on cleaning the place up." Kess motioned to the mess around them. The cabin's door had been completely ruined, and there were several holes in the walls where bullets had hit, not to mention the mud. After all the rain they'd been getting, by the time officers had processed the crime scene, there were muddy footprints everywhere. "We could've hired someone to do all this."

Curtis gave his sister what had to be some kind of sibling stare. "I wanted to make sure you at least got a new door up. It's bad enough you have to deal with that." He motioned to the blood stain that had soaked into the wooden floor where Victor had been shot. Scott, Kess's husband, had already called around and scheduled a professional to come tomorrow to clean it.

Rory took another sip of her tea. Kess had brought over

freshly baked chocolate chip cookies. She claimed part of her nesting phase during this pregnancy was to bake treats. Something Scott said he didn't object to.

"Were the kids excited to go over to your sister's house?"

Kess covered her mouth and finished her bite of cookie. "Oh, yes. Didn't even look back when we left." She rolled her eyes. "Scott and I are hoping to go away somewhere for the weekend before this little one is born." She lovingly patted her baby bump.

"The door is set." Scott stood back and admired their handiwork. "We'll have to install the security system, but that part can wait until after tomorrow."

Curtis snagged two cookies off the plate on the counter and handed one to Rory. "You should sit down for a little while. Get off your feet. You've already done a lot, and we don't want your headache coming back full force."

He was right. She was tired and could feel the beginning of one forming in her temple. "Yeah, that's a good idea." Rory took a spot on one end of the couch, and Curtis on the arm next to her.

"And you," Scott splayed his hand on his wife's belly, "need to rest so you don't overdo things."

"We need to mop the floor one more time to get the rest of the mud up."

"And I'll do that for you. Come on." He led her to a chair and then stood behind her and started rubbing her neck.

Kess nursed her glass of tea and looked from Rory to Curtis. "Have you heard how Braden's doing?"

Rory smiled at the thought of the little boy. "They removed his appendix. He's doing well and hopefully gets to go home tomorrow." She and Curtis had dropped by the hospital to see him earlier in the day.

Shelly had thanked Rory for taking care of her son and then apologized for the fact that they got caught up in everything.

Scott moved to sit on the other end of the couch from Rory. "Kess and I were talking about everything this morning, and we're still not clear on how everyone was connected in this case. Victor actually shot his brother? Why?"

Rory and Curtis had gone over the connections with Baker last night. Even now, the police were still trying to unravel the little details. She began at the beginning. "Victor and Greg's parents opened Hoops Artisan Jewelry over twenty-five years ago. Since then, he and his wife have built a name for themselves. What no one knew was that they used the jewelry store as a front for money laundering."

"And that the mall manager was in on the whole thing," Curtis added. "He was in charge of security, maintenance, and everything else that needed to be adjusted or tweaked to make sure the jewelry store was never questioned. In exchange, he received a percentage of the profits."

"Was Nolan the mall manager?"

"Not originally. But he took the job several years ago, not knowing what he was stepping into. Once he knew what was happening, Victor and Greg's father blackmailed him into turning a blind eye, insisting that his family would pay the price if he didn't."

Rory leaned forward and set her glass of tea on the coffee table. "It turns out their father had been grooming Victor to take over the business for years. Greg knew about it, but he wanted nothing to do with it. When their father died of a heart attack, he left the business to his sons since his wife was already struggling with Alzheimer's. Greg placed their mother in a really good assisted living facility but couldn't afford the payments on his own. Victor agreed to split the bill but only if Greg continued to work at the jewelry store."

Curtis moved from the arm of the couch to sit beside Rory. "We're not sure of the specifics, but the brothers had a lot of disagreements, and eventually Greg told Victor he wanted out of the family business and that he expected Victor to continue to help pay for their mother's medical care, or Greg was going to go to the police about the money laundering."

"Wow." Scott shook his head. "Is that when Victor decided they were a liability?"

Curtis nodded. "At the same time, Nolan was considering getting out of the business as well. Victor insisted that Nolan go with him to meet with a special client. That's when he stopped and killed Greg and Brenda. Nolan didn't pull the trigger, but he was there, and that's when Rory saw him in the woods. Victor threatened Nolan's family and reminded him that he was an accessory to murder."

"Victor blamed Nolan for my seeing his face," Rory added. "He told Nolan to take care of me before Nolan— and possibly Victor—were identified. Nolan wasn't a killer, though. He left the note and slashed my tires and burned the trailer hoping that I would be scared enough to leave town and solve the problem that way."

"What about the mall, though?" Kess pointed to the plate of cookies. Scott got one and handed it to her. "You saw him in the storm shelter, right?"

"Yes, I saw him. Victor caught him running and figured out what happened. He's the one who hit me with the fire extinguisher. I think that, if Curtis hadn't been there, he would've killed me." Rory leaned into Curtis.

He nudged her arm in return. "Victor originally had an alibi in place during the time of Greg and Brenda's death. But the security cameras in the jewelry store couldn't prove he was in his office. During the tornado warning, we realized there were back doors to every store that exited into those hallways. Victor could have easily snuck out of his store that way, and no one would've known."

Scott got another cookie and split it with his wife. "What's going to happen to Nolan?"

Curtis shrugged. "I don't think there's any way he'll stay out of jail. I mean, he was aware of the money laundering scheme for years and willingly took money to cover it up. But since he was under coercion when Greg and Brenda were killed, and he was ready to protect others when Victor came by the cabin, I think he'll receive some leniency. Still, he's going to miss a lot when it comes to his son's life."

Rory felt bad for Braden and Shelly. They truly didn't seem to realize what kind of business Nolan was into. "It's really sad. Three entire families were torn apart or destroyed. All over money."

The room was silent for several minutes as everyone finished their treats and considered the roller coaster ride of the last few days.

Finally, Kess leaned forward and addressed Rory. "You're welcome to stay as long as you'd like, until you find an apartment. I'll put you in a different cabin, though. And if you'd rather not, I more than understand."

Rory laughed. "I appreciate that. Thank you. And I'll take you up on the different cabin. I'll be okay if I don't see the inside of this one again anytime soon." Her gaze fell to the blood stain on the floor, then flitted to Curtis's face.

"Hopefully it won't be for very long. I'm going apartment hunting next week."

Kess whispered something to her husband who gave her a playfully exasperated look. "You're going to have to ask. Don't look at me."

Kess rolled her eyes. "Fine." She pointed to Rory and Curtis. "I have to ask, since the two of you aren't volunteering any information. Are you two together now? Because it kinda looks like you're a couple." She raised an eyebrow.

A flush crept up Rory's cheeks as her gaze met Curtis's. His expression mirrored a depth of feeling they hadn't yet voiced. Though their relationship was new, the thought of a future without him felt completely foreign.

Curtis reached for her hand and laced their fingers together. "Yeah, we are." He pressed a light kiss to the back of her hand. "Turns out we've both cared about each other for a while now. Better late than never."

Epilogue
Two Months Later

Rory reached for Curtis's hand as they approached his parents' house for dinner. Or at least that's what it was supposed to be. In reality, his mom was throwing a surprise birthday party for him several days before his actual birthday. She'd invited the whole family and sworn Rory to secrecy.

The problem was, while his mom might be good at keeping secrets, Curtis was way better at figuring them out.

"Remember, you promised you'd act surprised." Rory really didn't want his parents thinking she'd slipped and told him about the party.

Curtis parked the Jeep and swiveled to face her. "I promise." He leaned over and kissed her before releasing his seat belt and getting out of the Jeep with a groan.

He'd started the fire department's recruit academy last week, and he'd been sore and worn out by the end of every day. It'd been pushing him physically, and he'd been enjoying every minute of it.

He walked around the Jeep and opened Rory's door for

her. He lifted her left hand and ran his thumb over the engagement ring that sparkled in the sunlight. "Besides, we've got a little surprise of our own. Even if Mom does suspect I knew about the party ahead of time, this will more than make up for it."

She was a little nervous to tell everyone about their engagement, but most of all, she was excited about the idea of becoming part of such a big and loving family.

"Okay. I see someone watching out the window, so we'd better get in there, birthday boy." She slid her hand into his and leaned forward for one more kiss. "I love you."

He kissed her again. "I love you more."

Rory's heart swelled. She'd weathered a lot of storms in her life, but thanks to God's plans and the love of a man she adored, she'd never have to survive another one alone.

Special Thanks

I wanted to give a special shout out to Erynn Newman. Thank you SO much for working with me and my crazy schedule this time around. As always, your editing skills are fabulous. I appreciate you!

Heavenly Father, I'm especially thankful for all that You've accomplished in my life over the last few months. Your goodness and grace amaze me each and every day.

About the Author

Melanie D. Snitker is a *USA Today* bestselling author who writes inspirational romance and romantic suspense. She and her husband live in Texas with their two children. They share their home with three dogs and two terrariums filled with small critters. In her spare time, Melanie enjoys photography, reading, training her dog, playing computer games, and hanging out with family and friends.

https://www.melaniedsnitker.com/

Books by Melanie D. Snitker

Danger in Destiny

Out of the Ashes

Frozen in Jeopardy

Beneath the Surface

Caught in the Crosshairs

Running from the Past

In Search of the Truth

Assigned to Protect

Surviving the Storm

Forged by Fire

Brides of Clearwater

Marrying Mandy

Marrying Raven

Marrying Chrissy

Marrying Bonnie

Marrying Emma

Marrying Noel

Books by Melanie D. Snitker

Love's Compass Complete Series

Finding Peace

Finding Hope

Finding Courage

Finding Faith

Finding Joy

Finding Grace

Love Unexpected Complete Series

Safe In His Arms

Someone to Trust

Starting Anew

Healing Hearts

Calming the Storm

I Still Do

Don't Kiss Me Goodbye

Sage Valley Ranch

Charmed by the Daring Cowboy

Welcome to Romance

Fall Into Romance

A Merry Miracle in Romance